Everything We Hoped For

Everything We Hoped For

Pip Adam

Victoria University Press

TE WHARE WĀNANGA O TE ŪPOKO O TE IKA A MĀUI

VICTORIA
UNIVERSITY OF WELLINGTON

VICTORIA UNIVERSITY PRESS
Victoria University of Wellington
PO Box 600 Wellington
vup.victoria.ac.nz

National Library of New Zealand Cataloguing-in-Publication Data

Adam, Pip.
Everything we hoped for / Pip Adam.
ISBN 978-0-86473-625-3
I. Title.
NZ823.3—dc 22

Published with the support of a grant from

creative
nz
ARTS COUNCIL OF NEW ZEALAND *TOI AOTEAROA*

Printed by Yourbooks, Wellington

For Brent and Tallulah

Acknowledgements

Thanks to my friends and family for their support, the 2007 MA Class for their inspiration, Damien Wilkins for his thoughtful and insightful supervision, Jolisa Gracewood for sensitive and exacting editing, and Fergus Barrowman for his art and guidance.

Thanks for financial support to the donors of the IIML Project Scholarship

Several of these stories have previously been published in *Sport* and *Lumière Reader*.

Contents

A Bad Start

'Look at my watch.' The anaesthetist was holding his wrist so Ruth could read the time. The baby cried as the second hand struck eleven o'clock. 'It's a girl,' Nicholas said. As they lifted it over the screen Ruth saw it was hideous. A doctor took the baby away, leaving Ruth numb from the chest down, arms out like Jesus. Most of the people in the operating theatre followed the baby. Two surgeons stayed to sew up Ruth's stomach. She heard them say 'floppy uterus' more than once. She turned her head back to the anaesthetist and said, 'I'm going to be sick.' A nurse held a plastic container in front of Ruth's face. Nicholas came and sat beside her with the baby. It was screaming. He started to sing. 'I'm going to be sick,' Ruth told him. When the baby cried it sounded like something was squeezing it from deep inside. The midwife came to where Ruth's head was.

'I'm not staying here,' Ruth said. 'I want to go home.'

'You can't walk,' the midwife said.

'That's not my fault,' Ruth said.

'You have to stay here.'

'I want to go home.'

'Well,' the midwife stroked her hair, 'you can't walk, so you have to stay here.'

Ruth, Nicholas and the baby were the only people in the recovery room. It was late: the nurse had left. 'Get me more ice,' Ruth said. Nicholas took the polystyrene cup and filled it with ice from a small chilly bin near the nurses' desk. The baby sucked at Ruth and slept. Ruth crunched through the ice and said, 'Get me more ice.'

About an hour later, someone came and wheeled Ruth, the baby and the bed into an elevator, and then into a room. A nurse told Nicholas he had to go because Ruth wanted to sleep. There was another baby in the room, another woman, behind the curtain next to Ruth's bed. The other baby cried when Ruth's baby cried. Ruth rolled over; they'd put the baby in a small plastic box – like the fishbowls in primary school classrooms. She put her hand in the box and rubbed the baby's stomach. 'Shh,' she said, 'shh.' The baby stopped crying and Ruth rolled onto her back. 'What a bad start,' she said to the ceiling and to the baby and to herself.

Ruth's share of the room was still dull when the sun came up. The curtains cut her off from the other woman and the only window. More curtains cut her off from the wall, the sink, and the door that people came in and out of. The baby slept and Ruth lay on her back, still looking at the ceiling. Fluorescent tubes came on above her; the woman behind the curtain went to the bathroom and had a shower.

Someone wearing a white smock pulled the curtains back, looked at Ruth's catheter bag, lifted her sheets and said, 'Good grief. Someone should have changed these. Did no one change these?' Ruth shook her head. 'Your baby needs feeding.' The woman in the smock started winding the bed up. 'I know it's nice to have a rest but you need to wake that baby up and feed it.' She looked at Ruth's chart. 'Have you had pain relief?' Ruth wasn't sure. They'd given her an injection in her spine before the caesarean and there was a drip in her arm. The woman wrote something down and said, 'You should stand up and have a shower. You'll feel better once you're moving again.' While the woman changed the bloody sheets, Ruth stood like she was on a ledge, holding the tube for her catheter in one hand and the frame her drip hung on in the other. The baby slept. Ruth got back into bed and the woman checked her dressings. 'When you have a shower you need to take these off.' She meant the bandages. 'If you can't take them off, get one of the nurses to take them off. You can't have a shower until they take the catheter and the drip out.' The woman took the baby out of the plastic box and gave it to Ruth, saying, 'You need to feed the baby,' and then she went out, leaving the curtain open.

Ruth tried to remember the diagram from antenatal class. The one with the baby's cheek cut out so you could see the nipple in its mouth. She was pretty sure she was doing it wrong, but it would look right to anyone passing by the open door. Like the Madonna. She wasn't sure how long to feed the baby for, but every time it cried she really wanted to feed it and it cried every time it stopped sucking, so she kept feeding it. An hour later Nicholas arrived.

'You're feeding the baby,' he said.

'They say I have to have a shower and take the bandages off.'

'Oh.'

'I don't want to take the bandages off.'

'Have you stood up already?' He touched the back of the baby's head.

'Yeah, while they changed my bed. There was blood everywhere – it looked like something dreadful had happened.'

Nicolas nodded. 'How long have you been feeding her for?'

'A couple of hours.' Ruth arched her back.

'Have you had breakfast?'

'They won't give me anything to eat until I fart,' she said, 'to make sure they've put my bowels back in properly, or something.'

'Oh.' He looked up from the baby for the first time. 'So it's pretty much exactly as we dreamed.'

'Everything we hoped for,' she said.

They both laughed. Nicholas looked at the baby again, dropping his head from side to side. 'She's very cute, you know?' The baby had nodded off and was rubbing its face with its tiny hands.

'Her head's gone down a bit,' Ruth said, smoothing the place where the lump had been.

'And she's not blue,' Nicholas said.

There was a birthing pool set up in their spare room at home. They'd put it together when the baby was a week overdue; to cheer themselves up and give the baby some encouragement. Nothing happened. Ruth walked up hills, moved the refrigerator, ate curry. She did everything the midwife suggested. She and Nicholas had sex in a pragmatic way that felt, for the first time, like the sex their parents had explained to them as teenagers; this going here, that going there. When the baby was two weeks overdue the midwife sent them for a scan. The radiologist said, 'This is never coming out – it's huge.' Their midwife said, 'She shouldn't have said that. That's pretty unprofessional.'

Seventeen hours into the induced labour, the registrar said 'caesarean' in a sentence Ruth didn't hear the rest of. Ruth said to Nicholas, 'You talk to her, I can't talk to her, I'm not staying here another night.' He talked to the midwife, then came back and said Ruth and the baby had to stay at the hospital if there was a caesarean. Ruth said, 'There's a motel across the road. I'll stay there. Tell her that.' Nicholas went away, came back and said if there was a caesarean Ruth would have a catheter and a drip; she would have to stay in hospital with the baby.

Every time someone looked at Ruth's chart they said, 'Failure to progress,' and, 'Have you had pain relief?' Nicholas made notes on the back of his hand with a pen because Ruth couldn't remember and no one who worked at the hospital seemed to know. That afternoon, someone took out the drip and the catheter, but not before Nicholas's father visited and made a joke about the

13

bag hanging off the side of Ruth's bed. Nicholas held the baby and walked around the room while Ruth went to the shower and looked at the bandages. She had no idea what was under them. She was sore. She couldn't imagine being more sore. She left them on. There was a laundry bag in the bathroom; Ruth put her hospital gown in it and put on the clothes Nicholas had brought in for. Her own clothes.

'Is that better?' Nicholas said.

'Yeah, heaps.'

That evening one of the nurses said the baby wasn't getting enough food. 'It needs formula.' Ruth said no. 'Well, you'll have to express, to try and speed things up.' The nurse went away and came back with a syringe without a needle and a diagram showing how to hand-express. It was like milking a cow and being a cow at the same time. Ruth sucked a tiny amount of watery colostrum into the syringe. The nurse took Nicholas and showed him where to put it in the ward fridge. Ruth dozed, and when the baby woke up said, couldn't Nicholas go and get the stuff from the fridge and give it to the baby so she could sleep some more. He went and came back and said someone had taken it. Someone else's baby was drinking Ruth's milk.

At home, around the birthing pool, they'd put pillows and a CD player. She would have the baby, then they would all crawl into bed for a couple of days. Feeding, eating, staying warm. People would visit them. They would hang a sign up when they were sleeping and people wouldn't visit them. No one that visited would drink her breast milk.

Around ten thirty a nurse came and told Nicholas to go home and took Ruth's bandages off. The baby woke up, crying. Ruth fed the baby for another three or four hours. The woman behind the curtain shouted out for Ruth to keep the baby quiet because it was waking up her baby. Ruth took the baby and the blanket her mother had knitted and went to the television lounge. There was a vampire movie on. The baby dozed in her arms. Ruth walked slowly back to her room and put the baby in the plastic crib. She got herself into bed and shut her eyes. The baby woke up half an hour later. The woman behind the curtain made a disapproving noise. Ruth went back to the television lounge and fed her baby in the dark illuminated by the television. As the night went on, the baby started to talk to Ruth, saying 'No' when she took it off her breast. It was a boy, then a girl, then a tiny strange monkey who had lost a hat or a glove.

A nurse came and told her she needed to go back to her room. It wasn't good for the baby to be up all night watching television. Ruth said the baby was disturbing the other woman in the room. The nurse said she couldn't be afraid of other people. It was her room and she needed to stay there. Ruth went back to her room. The baby cried and the woman said, 'Be quiet,' so Ruth snuck out of the room, out of the ward and walked the baby up and down in the foyer by the outpatient clinic. When she came back, the door to the ward was locked. There was a phone by the door; she lifted it to her ear. A nurse answered. She told Ruth she couldn't just leave the ward; they'd been looking for her, where had she been?

'Can I go home?' Ruth asked.

'If you're asking whether you can discharge yourself,' the nurse on the other end of the phone said, 'we wouldn't advise it, but we couldn't do anything about it if that's what you decided you wanted to do and there are plenty of people who would be happy to have your bed.'

'Can you bring my clothes out?' Ruth asked.

'You can't discharge yourself now, it's late. You have to wait until morning.'

The door made a clicking noise and opened out toward Ruth. She and the baby went back into the ward and sat in the dark in the television room. She watched the baby until the sun came up. It wriggled slowly, like it was struggling to get out of something. It scrunched up its nose and every time it opened its eyes it looked like it had woken up on a bus, or at work, or somewhere it didn't expect to wake up. Ruth held its hand and found a plastic bracelet on its wrist. 'Baby of Ruth Spencer,' she read. It was true – she'd seen the baby come out of her body and it hadn't left her since. And now it stretched and started nuzzling into her, looking for food.

The Kiss

At six o'clock on the morning of the sixteenth of December, the soldiers of Echo Company woke in Dili, showered, dressed in civilian clothes and made their way to the vehicles that would take them to the plane that would take them home. There was towel-flicking and a shared feeling of excitement and joy. They had packed the night before and their rifles would travel separately. In Darwin they changed planes and boarded an Air New Zealand flight. They laughed at the safety instructions, ate small bags of peanuts and drank complimentary beer. Several air hostesses declined to give their phone numbers. The flight home was noisy; there were jokes and horse-play, head-rubbing and play-fighting. In all the noise a few soldiers looked out the windows at the clouds and felt their eyelids drop.

As the plane flew over Canterbury some of the men shouted out landmarks that became apparent as they continued their descent. From the plane they could see the airport and a large sign saying 'Christchurch'. They couldn't see the crowd of family and friends in the arrival area, but they felt it. On the ground, and as the seat-belt sign went off, they felt the weight of the people waiting for them. They disembarked, saying thank you to the air hostesses.

Before the doors through to the arrival area there was a duty-free shop. The first off the plane stopped at the shop and the others, one by one, five by five, fell in. Recognisable as soldiers by their short haircuts and tidy jeans, they tried on sunglasses and looked at bottles of spirits. The married soldiers sniffed perfumes and asked the women behind the counter about them. Three soldiers, almost the last off the plane, stood at the entrance of the shop until they saw another soldier looking at a shelf of aftershave. Wyatt, a broad man who wanted to be a chef and was everyone's first pick for anything needing weight and force, joked that even the most expensive aftershave wouldn't help the soldier have sex with anything resembling a woman. The others laughed. They started looking at the aftershaves, joking about the names, spraying each other with the testers. Lennon wore his glasses. Knight, the third man, called him 'my blind foot-soldier' when they were on patrol. Lennon said he was fine unless it was raining or humid which, Wyatt pointed out, was all the time in East Timor. Knight said, 'Exactly, a blind assassin – stay in front of me.' The first soldiers stayed as long as possible, then began to disperse into the arrival area. The soldiers left in the duty-free shop heard the shouts and cheers and screams of excitement. They looked toward them as the shop fell silent for a moment.

As they walked through, Wyatt was grabbed by his mother and sisters who met him with kisses and hugs, whoops, small jumps and claps. Knight was met by several women who called themselves his good friends; they hugged and kissed him, except the ones who were in the army as well, these women stood back, shook his hand, then walked into sportsfield hugs. They thought this meant more than thrusting their chests forward and wet-kissing his cheek. Knight didn't.

Lennon was the last to come through the double doors, his mother was there. His girlfriend ran to him, grabbed his face in both hands and kissed him on the mouth. She looked odd. He'd forgotten about her. He'd seen her name on the letters she sent, called her a couple of times. He'd mentioned her name and had her name mentioned to him in strip bars and mess tents but he'd forgotten about her – the her that stood in front of him now, smiling broadly and wiping tears away like something he was sure she'd seen on television. She was something waiting for him – what could be done with her now? He kept his distance. Lennon wasn't frightened of anything but he kept his distance, unsure of what she could tell or smell or sense. He smiled at her carefully from beside his mother. Wyatt and Knight came over and said something about a party in the afternoon. Wyatt was going to have breakfast with his family and Knight said he was going to have sex with one, or more, of the women. They left.

Eventually everyone left. Lennon kept saying, I just need to see so-and-so, and ducking off, but eventually everyone had left and he was there with them so he said, 'Shall we go for some breakfast? I could murder some food.' He would travel with his girlfriend, his mother would come in her own car.

On the way to the restaurant there was a long silence. Lennon put his hand on his girlfriend's thigh and said, 'Good to see you.' She said, 'Oh Mike.' He didn't have to say anything else or touch her again for the rest of the journey.

They talked at breakfast, told him someone had died, someone else had got married and the weather had been warmer than last year. Did he like his mother's new haircut? It was shorter. Lennon ate and looked at his watch and the clock on the wall behind his girlfriend. He paid the bill and met them in the car park. His mother said goodbye. He thought he would mess around in town until the party but his girlfriend held out her car keys and asked if he wanted to drive. She meant back to her place, to drop his stuff off, and he realised she expected him to stay there. He was going to crash at the party or catch a lift back to barracks but he didn't tell her that. It could still turn out that way, but not if he told her. He hadn't driven for nearly a year. He'd been awake for almost twenty-four hours, travelled hundreds of kilometres and she wanted him to drive, so she could feel like a war-bride. It would get him into town and there wouldn't be a fight. Concurrent activity, he thought, eating and marching. It was money in the bank, easy money.

At her flat he took another, longer shower and dressed in the humid dampness of the bathroom – blind. She offered to take him to the party and he said no, Wyatt was picking him up. She said okay, and looked out the window. He told her not to start and she said sorry, it's just that he only just got home. He said just don't fucking start and she said yeah, she wouldn't start, she had stuff to do. She had no money. He could tell. She was listed as a dependant on his record. They'd lived together for a year in the army housing area. She'd left while he was in Bougainville for a week. She'd taken lots but left more. She took the cat. Weeks later, when they were back together, it had to be put down after it broke a hip. She got another cat. He offered to look after it when she moved into this place. He told her to get a collar on it because they shot cats in barracks and she'd said he had to keep it inside for a couple of weeks. It disappeared within days and she didn't say anything about it. He suspected she was saving it up and about a month before he went to East Timor he was right. He'd wanted to go out for dinner and a movie with someone and she said she didn't think it was appropriate for him to go. He said he was going and don't start, and she said, 'What about the cat?' He took forty dollars out of his jeans pocket and left it beside the basin for her. She'd put on weight. Shitloads of weight. Every time he went away she put on weight. When he got back she put on more. She looked fat. One thing about Indonesian women – they weren't fat.

Wyatt arrived fifteen minutes prior to parade with Knight in the back seat, slightly drunk in the arms of one of the women from the airport; she was also quite drunk. Lennon saw his girlfriend see the woman with Knight and as she opened her mouth to say something he said, 'She's a hooker. It's only strippers and hookers at the party.' As he jumped in the front seat his girlfriend told him to text her and she'd meet him in town and something else as Wyatt drove him away from her.

In the car Knight said the woman he was with gave good head. She hit him on the arm and sat slightly taller. Wyatt asked how was brunch and he and Lennon laughed, saying 'Fuuuuck!' and shaking their heads. What was up with them, they asked. It was doing Lennon's head in, he said, and Wyatt agreed it was also doing his head in. Knight said a surf would be good as they passed the beach and Lennon said surfing was a pussy sport and Knight was a pussy. Knight said it was better to be a pussy than pussy-whipped like, for instance, Lennon. Lennon leaned over and slapped him. Knight slapped him back. Lennon told Knight not to make him come over there and turned back to the front of the car. There were people on the golf course, men and women playing golf like it was an ordinary Saturday afternoon. Wyatt pulled into the mall at Shirley so they could all buy alcohol. Knight bought the woman a lollipop. The mall was full of people doing their Christmas shopping. Tinsel and snow hung off everything. The woman with Knight stopped to try on sunglasses and said, 'Buy me some sunglasses, Knight.' Lennon said, 'Buy me some sunglasses, Knight,' and told Knight to sort it out, for Christ's sake. Knight said quietly to Lennon that he, Lennon, didn't understand just how good the head was she gave and handed her a fifty-dollar note. The woman kissed Knight on the cheek, took the money and, while the men were in the bottle store, didn't buy sunglasses.

The party was on Bealey Avenue, a long road with tall trees along the middle of it. It was daylight when they arrived. On the front lawn of the row of flats Hohepa was chasing Singer and Foster was yelling at Patchett. Some other soldiers were sitting in the sun, drinking. Wyatt, Knight and Lennon nodded at the men on the lawn and Knight, with his arm round the woman, tried to catch Singer as he ran past. Singer yelled something like 'pussy' at him, so Knight joined Hohepa in the chase. The woman who was with Knight stood and laughed and opened one of Knight's beers and drank it.

Inside the flat the curtains were drawn and the stereo played loud music. There were soldiers in every room; lying on couches, sitting on the floor – all drinking. The host, Woodhead, was in the kitchen with his hand up his girlfriend's skirt. When he saw Lennon and Wyatt arrive he smiled and slapped them on the back. His girlfriend pulled down her skirt and emptied a bag of chips into a bowl. Woodhead led them to the living room where they were welcomed with a volley of hoots. Someone made room for them on the couch and they sat and drank and no one said much to anyone except quotes from *Full Metal Jacket* and *Starship Troopers*. When it finally got dark, the lounge was cleared a bit and the strippers arrived. Woodhead's girlfriend and the woman with Knight joined in. Lennon was offered several women but said he was home now and everyone said 'pussy-whipped' and pretended to be on leashes. Woodhead's girlfriend chose one of the strippers and Woodhead said for everyone to look after themselves for a couple of hours. Someone shouted more like a couple of minutes and Woodhead emptied the bottle he was drinking from and threw it so it hit the wall and exploded.

Around nine, Lennon's cell phone rang. It was his girlfriend. He sighed and let it ring. He turned and asked if Wyatt wanted to go into town. Wyatt said sure, maybe, in a bit. Lennon stood up and went down the hall to find a quiet room to ring her back. The first one he tried had people in it, and the second, but the third was empty and dark. He closed the door behind him, keeping it dark, and rested his weight on the door. Sudden movement coming toward him startled Lennon. The man, who he couldn't make out, said, 'You came.' Hands pulled Lennon's face close and kissed him. The hands held his head, his neck, his jaw, pulling him closer and further into the kiss. Then pulled back and pushed Lennon away. Cold rushed in. Lennon's phone rang green and illuminated but the man was gone. Lennon closed his eyes and felt it all over him, again and again – the stillness of the room. Quiet and alone – it was all he wanted. Someone was calling his name from another room, Wyatt, asking where the fuck he was and had anyone seen Lennon.

Although the rest of the house was only dimly lit, it was blinding. The right thing occurred to Lennon – to run from the room shouting that some faggot tried to kiss him. All eyes were on him, saying Wyatt's looking for you and slapping him, shouting 'pussy-whipped' and saying she could smell him up to no good. Wyatt was with Knight when Lennon found him, on the front lawn holding his cell phone to his ear. When Lennon saw them he wiped his mouth with the back of his hand. It took him like falling – the sensation that hung on him pushed deep inside, filling him, trying to escape out every pore. Wyatt raised his eyes, pushed the phone into Lennon's chest and told him to fucking sort it out. It was her. She'd tried his phone and couldn't get through so she'd called the barracks and someone had given her Wyatt's cell number. Lennon looked at the empty sky. He said way to much: he'd been trying to call her from a quiet room but she was engaged so he'd stayed there for a bit and tried again and dozed off. She wanted to meet him in town. She was out with a few friends. Did he want to meet at this bar? Wyatt was standing beside him drinking his last beer. Lennon asked if he wanted to go to the bar. Wyatt said sure, yeah. Knight said, 'Don't fucking humour him, he's got to sort that bitch out.' Wyatt said he was out of beer so he needed to go somewhere and Knight could talk – where was his missus? Knight said she wasn't his missus and he told her to go home when he found her and Woodhead's missus having sex with about ten guys watching. Wyatt pissed himself laughing. Knight said he would go to the bar, not because he wanted to but to show Wyatt what a fuckwit he was, and that he, Knight wouldn't be alone for long, but Wyatt would be alone forever. Wyatt said he would rather be alone forever than not get invited to his girlfriend's live sex show. Knight said shut up and for fuck's sake hurry up, Lennon, if they were going let's fucking go, for Christ's sake.

Lennon got off the phone and handed it back to Wyatt without saying anything. They began to walk away from the party when Wyatt said, 'Where's your fucking jacket, Lennon?' Lennon had taken it off inside somewhere. He walked back over the lawn, picking his way over the soldiers who were lying there. On patrol, at night, no one slept until it was their turn and then they slept well.

During the day, through the strangle of bush, each man watched the one directly in front, never needing to look back or to the side. When the militia opened fire, they retreated and hid together in the small spaces they found down low and were quiet. He should find the faggot and tear him apart. Patchett and Singer leant on either side of the door, beers in hand. They nodded and met his eye. There were soldiers everywhere inside. He had to push past to get to the lounge. They were pushing on him, leaning on him, heavy and drunk. He said sort it out a few times and with every push on him his body swam and the margins where his skin stopped broke like shrapnel had opened them. When the shooting stopped several of them were crying. They crawled out of their low places to find Deering missing. Lennon's body was leaking out his skin and the pushing and the leaning was leaking into him. Washing in like a tide and he was getting fuller and fuller and could feel every pore of the skin on his face.

Miller was on his jacket, a topless woman in a G-string was on Miller. Lennon leaned down to pull his jacket out and his cheek grazed the woman's breast. He turned and kissed it. She held his head close to her. Someone grabbed his arm; it was Wyatt come to see where he'd got to. Lennon turned quickly. Wyatt looked him in the eye and said, 'Have you got your jacket?' Lennon looked around to make sure no one else had seen and pulled his jacket out from under Miller. On the way out Lennon's girlfriend called Wyatt's phone again and he told her they were on their way and they would be about half an hour. As he hung up he told her to lose his fucking number. Knight met them outside and asked where the fuck Lennon had got to. Wyatt raised his eyes and said let's walk to the bar.

They walked and kicked things and jumped over things and hit things but none of them were looking for a fight. Lennon's phone rang but he didn't answer it. Wyatt said, 'Oh fuck, Lennon, she'll just call me – for fuck's sake.' Lennon said, 'All right' and told them to go ahead and pretended to answer his phone. Knight said, 'I'd do her.' Wyatt looked at him like you've got to be joking and Knight said, 'She must be fucking amazing for Lennon to put up with all this shit.' They both laughed and Lennon caught up with them.

'Makes you want to go to war,' Wyatt said. Knight laughed and Lennon looked around and said he'd get the drinks. There were dress pants everywhere; men their age with stupid civvy haircuts drinking stupid drinks and chatting up ugly hairdressers and sales assistants. The doorman had said he didn't want any trouble. Knight said, 'Mate, there's only three of us.' The doorman had let them in, repeating he didn't want any trouble. It all operated below them – everything that goes on. Broken shoelaces, lost jobs, car insurance. Not by choice. It was just where they lived now – a couple of feet above it all. Lennon's girlfriend waved at him as he waited at the bar.

Back at her flat, in the dark of her bedroom, Lennon went down on her and she came. Then they fucked and he came. He held her as she got heavier and heavier and then he went to the kitchen to get a drink. He opened the fridge and something fell off the door. It was a magnet he'd sent her from Bali; a carved wooden fish. He turned it over with his foot. The note he'd sent with it was on the floor as well. She'd cut it out like a speech bubble and stuck it to the front of the fish with Sellotape. He didn't need to read it because he knew what it said. A car went past outside on the street and he caught himself in the reflection of the glass door, skinny and naked and spent. He could leave. People left people all the time but he wanted her to go. He tried to make it complicated, but it wasn't. He picked up his clothes and got dressed. The door was deadlocked. His girlfriend walked toward the bathroom, naked and rubbing her face. She looked at Lennon and said, 'They're by the phone' and closed the bathroom door.

It was a clear night. The sun would be up in a few hours; until then he would walk around. He'd get some breakfast and call Wyatt for a ride out to barracks. It was what he'd wanted from the start. It was all he ever wanted. He walked past houses and pubs and through a cemetery until he came to the river. He sat beside it and watched it move. The air was still and held his face. As the dark water bit at the shore he ran every man's face through his mind. Trying to match jaws with the one that had touched his. He thought of their hands and then their hands holding their rifles. He eliminated some, shivering in the pre-dawn. He could feel the indent of those hands on the back of his neck. The light had fallen on Deering's face. It shouldn't have but after they'd looked and looked, in a place that was previously dull, a light fell on Deering's calm, still face, where he lay alone and quiet. Knight had said, 'For fuck's sake' and turned away. Wyatt had vomited, resting his whole body-weight on his rifle as he bent over. Out of all of them, Lennon wished it was

Deering. He ran through every man's torso, their chests. He mixed torsos with faces and hands. Someone's right hand with another's left – Deering's head three feet from the rest of him. Carrying him back to camp, holding his head, his neck, his jaw. He went over it all. Trying to remember every time he had touched or been touched by someone in Echo Company.

When Lennon arrived back at Woodhead's flat there were still soldiers everywhere, asleep now. He walked through the house, through room after room of sleeping soldiers until he found the room where it had happened. It was still empty. He closed the door behind him. The first of the dawn broke through the Venetian blinds as he lay on the bed. He balanced on the edge of sleep and felt the weight of everything above him – gravity pushing it down on him. That faggot was bound to come back and when he did Lennon would kill him. Something wrong until now slipped and was almost right. Everything rose in him as he remembered. In his mind he heard Deering breathe – in and out. He breathed in what was left of it. He thought about the fish and the note and how much he'd meant it when he wrote it. From the bottom of his heart he'd meant it and for what he imagined was forever.

This Is Better

The guy says to me, 'How much is this?' He's holding a set of three plastic boats, cocooned in more plastic and backed in cardboard.

'It's $1.95,' I say.

He looks at the boats and nods. He's a mystery shopper. I'm unpacking glass orbs with coloured bubbles in them and putting them on a low shelf. I'm on my knees.

'What about those?' he says, pointing with the boats at the glass things I'm unpacking.

'These ornaments,' I say, 'are also $1.95.' I don't look at him but I imagine him nodding and pursing his lips like he's trying to act out 'That's a good deal' without any words, like he's trapped behind something see-through and soundproof.

I hear it before he asks, the inhale he makes so he can say, 'What about those coffee mugs over there, how much are those?'

I look up to where he's pointing and say at the same time, before I actually see the coffee mugs, 'Those coffee mugs are also $1.95. Everything in this store is $1.95.' And he nods again. He comes on the last Wednesday of the month and usually I'm on my knees or up a step ladder or reaching under something and always he asks how much three things cost and usually he asks me, because Lee tells him to, because although I get it right, he can't quite put his finger on it, so he says to the guy, 'Something not right – can you put your finger on it?' and I figure, because the guy keeps asking me, he can't.

In the town we live in there are fifty thousand people. It feels like all of them shop in this store a couple of times a week, except the guy who comes in on the last Wednesday of the month and asks how much three things cost and buys three things and pays for them with a fifty-dollar note and asks whoever serves him what time we shut and always comes in when it's quiet and always asks Steve, as he's leaving, if we're getting any new stock and always comes back and asks Dave how one thing works. No one talks about it. No one talks about it to me. Sometimes I lose it a bit, around my eyes, I feel my eyes squint a bit because I can't always believe it, that's why I try not to look at him. I look at the space between his eyes once and then don't look at him again. They can't put their finger on it so they can't fault me on it.

I can see Lyall watching it all, from the counter. I can almost feel him thinking, 'Please don't fuck up.' I'm his 100% man but he still looks at me like he's thinking, 'Please don't fuck up,' and when I make eye contact with him he looks quickly at the counter like he wasn't watching and

31

everything is just carrying on as usual, despite the fact he's looking at an empty counter like he's praying – he's gone from begging to praying. He needs the manager's mystery-shopper bonus. He needs it every month. He has a couple of kids and a wife and a house but he needs it in some other messy way he thinks he's hiding. Every month after the mystery-shopper report comes in Lyall comes up to me and pats me on the back and says, 'Lloyd, well done.' Lyall is six months older than me. At the moment, we're both thirty-three.

The phone rings. Lyall says, 'Lloyd, can you get that?' He's standing beside the phone and I have to stand up, climb over some boxes and walk across the store to answer it.

'Hello, *Dollar Ninety-Five Store*, Lloyd speaking. Can I help you?'

'Oh, hello.' It's the guy. In the reflection of the glass cabinet that's sitting on the counter I can see him with a cell phone on the street outside the shop. My eyes squint a little bit. 'I was wondering if you could tell me what you sell?'

'Sure,' I say, 'we sell almost everything: toys, stationery and craft supplies, kitchen utensils, make-up and beauty supplies, and it's all only $1.95.'

'That's great,' he says.

'It is,' I say. I think I can hear myself in his cell phone, like an echo. 'Is there anything else I can help you with today?'

'No,' he says, 'I think that's everything.'

It's almost lunchtime; Lee and Nancy will be in any minute. I hang up the phone and I'm still holding one of the orbs and I notice for the first time that the bubbles have eyes, like they're fish or one-celled organisms. I hold it up to the light coming in the front door from the street. It's a bright, cold day.

'They've got eyes,' I say.

Lyall looks up and for a second we look at the eyes in the bubbles in the orb together.

'It's flat on the bottom,' I say turning it over a bit. 'I guess it's for your desk or something.'

Lyall moves away from me and says, 'You should probably get them unpacked,' nodding toward the box and the shelf, 'before lunch.' At the same time he reaches for a piece of paper which he puts in front of him on the counter and looks at.

'Yeah,' I say, and I go back to unpacking again.

Lee and Nancy arrive at lunchtime. It gets busy at lunchtime. From the door Lee says they've come to watch their money coming in. He says it like it's a joke and we all smile and Lyall laughs. I call them Lee and Nancy. Everyone knows, but I still call them Lee and Nancy and smile when Lee makes jokes about money and being weak and things like that. There are still some boxes lying around and Steve has about a dozen lip gloss sets to hang up on moveable hooks that are precarious until the weight on them is just right. I grab the boxes and Dave goes to help Steve. Lyall runs to help Lee with the stock he's carrying and trips heavily on something. 'You right, Lyall?' Lee says. 'Watch it big guy.' He slaps Lyall on the back and they both laugh again.

Most people in the town we live in work for Nancy

and Lee. Not so much in the store but in the warehouse and driving the trucks and in the office. The idea was so simple and although they have three hundred franchisees nationwide they like to run everything from here. Lee likes the beach and Nancy likes her friends. They keep the international airport running. If you asked a class of sixteen-year-olds at our high school, a quarter of them would say, 'Going to university,' and three quarters of them would say, 'Working for Lee and Nancy.' If you asked them a year later, they would all be working for Nancy and Lee, or training to work for Lee and Nancy, or wanting a job with Nancy and Lee.

Lyall went to university for two years. If you asked him he would tell you he was head-hunted. Lyall and I used to go to school together. The day he had his interview at the *Dollar Ninety-Five Store*, Lee and Nancy called Steve and Dave and me over and Nancy said, 'Fellas, this is Lyall, he's your new manager.' Then they showed him round and he left the store and came back a couple of minutes later. He couldn't have gotten any further than the corner and he found me in the shop, up a three-step ladder and said he wanted to concentrate on his career and that's why he'd come back. I looked down at him and said, 'Sure.' It was the first thing he'd said to me in two and a half years. He said he doubted he would be back for long. That was thirteen years ago.

'Hi everyone,' says Nancy as she comes in the door. We all say, 'Hi,' and she says, louder, 'I said *Hi everyone*,' and we all say, 'Hi,' a bit louder. 'That's better,' she says, and to someone who's just come in the shop, 'Isn't that better?' The woman with the pram nods and Nancy says,

'I thought I was at the morgue. Let's get some energy into this shop,' and she walks around the shop touching just about everything on the shelves.

She stands behind Steve, who is balancing the lip glosses on the hooks and says, 'Hi Steve.'

'Hi Nancy,' Steve says, turning at an odd angle to look her in the face.

'Those glosses look great. We are going to sell some of those today, aren't we Steve?'

'We sure are, Nancy,' Steve says.

'We sure are,' says Nancy as she continues round the shop, touching things and adjusting things and looking at where the light is falling on things. 'Hi Lloyd,' she says.

'Hi Nancy,' I say. She's standing right in front of me. She's caught me just standing.

'Well, Lloyd, I can hardly hear you, I said, *Hi Lloyd*.'

'Hi Nancy,' I say louder, and I smile.

'That's better Lloyd. My, but don't those glass novelties look grand. Lyall, don't these glass novelties look grand?'

Lyall nods and says, 'Sure do, Nancy.'

'Well done, Lloyd,' says Nancy.

I smile and nod. There's nothing in her eyes.

'They're flat on the bottom,' I say, picking one up to show her.

'Well done, Lloyd,' she says and turns away and continues round the shop touching things.

We used to fight a lot. We would shout at each other and after a while she would shout, 'I'm happy Lloyd. Can you say that?' and I couldn't and I can't.

The shop gets really busy. There's a bit of a queue and Lee starts handing out sweets and 10 per cent off vouchers.

The glass orbs all but sell out and Lee gets Steve to get some more out of the box he brought in and those go too, people are buying three and four of them at a time. People are buying the lip gloss sets as well and the balance tips and the ones that are left on the hook fall on the floor. As Steve's picking them up, people take them out of his hands and off the floor and they all go. People come to the counter with boxes of boats and coffee mugs and cheese graters and pen sets and pen sets for their fridges and caps and socks and colouring books and the cash register rings and the bags snap open and crackle shut. Then almost as fast as it started it's quiet in the shop again. Steve and Lyall take the first lunch break and I go and tidy up the shop while Dave counts the cash to do a change order.

Lee says, like he's giving a speech, 'Oh, well, we should be off then, Nancy. Flying visit lads,' and he smiles like his eyes are busy doing something different.

'Right you are, Lee,' Nancy says.

Lee has to pass me to leave the store and as he does he says, as low as he can, 'Dinner's at six. Your mother's planning something nice, so don't be late.'

I nod and say, 'Thanks, Lee.'

They like to keep me close and we don't fight any more. I go to work and I come home from work and we have dinner at seven and always my mother plans something nice and I go out with Lee on Thursdays, or when there's a rugby match, for a drink, and I smile and I listen and I watch and Lee drinks and says things like, 'One day all this will be yours,' and we smile at each other and he pats me on the back and he drinks some more and says, when he thinks no one else can hear, 'This is better.

Isn't this better, Lloyd?' and I say, 'Yeah, this is better, Lee,' and pat him on the arm and finish my beer and take him home. Every day I try to find something to fascinate me or something that used to fascinate me or something that might fascinate me at some point in the future. It's like being a stamp collector in a digital age.

Lee slaps Lyall on the back again as he leaves, and whispers something in his ear, and they laugh again. It occurs to me I've known Lyall longer than I haven't known him. He's walking back toward the counter shaking his head and he says to Steve, 'That Lee,' and he takes the paper Steve's been working on and checks his sums for the change request. He's still laughing and shaking his head and saying, under his breath, 'That Lee.' Lee says things like 'camp as a row of tents' and 'useless as tits on a bull' and 'dry as a nun's cunt', and all these things make Lyall laugh. Lee and Nancy often go for dinner at Lyall and his wife's house. Lyall's wife is called Michele. I imagine what those dinners must be like. Lee making jokes and Lyall laughing so much he can't get a word out. I imagine him laughing and laughing until his sides hurt and he's crying and the only words he can get out are, 'Lee, stop. Please, stop.' Nancy and Michele in the kitchen. I have no idea what women talk about when they're in a room together. In my imagination they get dessert and talk about children and shoes – the things I know about children and shoes. Lyall and I used to spend every hour we could together. When people ask me how well I know Lyall, I say, 'Not very.'

*

The mystery-shopper report comes in. The guy from the warehouse who brings boxes of new stock hands it to Lyall in an envelope. While Steve and Dave and I check the stock in the boxes against the invoices Sellotaped to the lids of the boxes, Lyall takes the envelope to the counter, opens it and reads the report. As we're unpacking the stock, Steve says to Dave, 'Wow, what cool new stuff,' and Steve replies, 'Yeah, we are going to sell some of these egg slicers.' I laugh and go to look up and they're not laughing and I say ,'Yeah,' and stop smiling and nod. There are four boxes. When they're empty I pick them up, one under each arm and the other two in my hands. I open the door at the back of the store with my foot and go into the alley to the caged skip where we put the boxes and the paper and the packaging the stock comes in. I drop the boxes and they make a hollow bang. None of the sun at the front of the shop gets into the alley. It's grey and cold and quiet. I pull the lid of one of the boxes and the glue gives way and I flatten it and throw it into the cage of the skip.

When I get back inside the store Lyall is talking to Steve and Dave and holding the mystery-shopper report. When I reach them Lyall puts his arm around me and pats my shoulder. 'Look at this, Lloyd,' he says and shows me the report and it says we did good. 'Well done, Lloyd,' he says, and takes his arm from round me. 'Well done all of us.' He walks toward the counter. 'This deserves an afternoon tea.' He picks up the phone and calls Michele. Steve and Dave and I go to separate corners of the store to count the stock and check the stock is facing out. 'Hi honey,' Lyall says. 'Look, we just got a great mystery-shopper report down here at the store and I was wondering if you could bring us down something nice for afternoon tea.' He has his hands in his hair and he's looking out the front door. 'Great. You're great. Half two? Thanks honey. Love you, too.'

It was all about timing. If they'd come in earlier, Lee and Nancy would have seen the truth of it and Lyall wouldn't have been able to do what he did; he would have been forced to do something different. But they didn't. We were supposed to be at school and they were supposed to be at work but they came in and the room smelt like sex and it looked like sex and I was stripped to the waist and Lyall was dressed and Lee said, 'What the fuck is going on?' and Lyall went to leave and I said, 'Don't leave, Lyall.' He kept leaving and I held him and said, just to him, with my face buried in his hair, 'You don't have to leave,' like this was the moment when all the hiding stopped and our families stood around us and held us in our joy.

In my memory, usually, it's slow, like time stopped and Lyall had hours to mull it over and think about the pros and cons and travel into the future, to a time when he has a girlfriend pregnant by accident and he has to come home from university and he needs a job and Lee and Nancy employ just about everyone. And then time starts again and he punches me and shouts, 'You fucking faggot,' and leaves and gets a girlfriend and goes to university.

When I looked up Lee was shaking his head and everything had gone from Nancy's eyes.

I make up a scene which explains everything. Lyall comes to Lee and Nancy the night after he punches me and explains he was trying to help but it can't go on so he has to stay away. Lee says he understands and Nancy says it's a fine thing he's doing to help out a friend in need. This is what she says to me when the fighting starts – 'It's a noble thing Lyall is doing.'

But, sometimes, in my memory, it happens quick – lightning quick.

Michele comes into the store with a carrot cake and one of Lyall's children, probably the youngest. He kisses her and the child on the cheek and he takes the cake. Michele says, 'Hi Steve,' and, 'Hi Dave,' and, 'Hi Lloyd,' and we all say, 'Hi,' and I say, 'Can you stay for afternoon tea, Michele?' and she says, 'No' almost before I've finished and she kisses Lyall again and leaves, carrying the child on one of her hips. Lyall says, 'Steve, you be mother' and hands him the cake and Steve goes to the staff room and boils the jug and one by one we go into the staff room, which is only big enough for one of us at a time, and we have a cup of milky tea and a slice of carrot cake with cream cheese icing which Lyall says Michele whipped up in between looking after the children and keeping the house tidy and then he tells a joke Lee told him about why brides wear white and Dave and I laugh. Steve's in the staff room having a second slice of cake.

It gets slow in the shop, really slow, and Lyall has us take all the eye shadow sets and nail polish bottles off the hooks and put them closer to the counter because he says he's worried about shoplifters. Steve and Dave leave at about three and Lyall and I are in the shop by ourselves for an hour or so. It gets darker outside and some lights come on in the street. Lyall stands at the counter looking at bits of paper and phoning Lee, and I clean the shelves.

40

I take everything off the shelves, spray glass cleaner on, wipe it off and then put everything back on the shelves. Every now and then someone comes in and looks around and either buys something or asks me where something is.

Lyall always sends me home at twenty-five minutes past five. He says something like, 'You might as well get going, Lloyd.' I say something like, 'Okay,' and I get my jacket and my bag and I say, 'Bye.' It's to give me a head start. Otherwise we would have to walk part of the way together. I get paid until five thirty. I don't think he's told Lee. That's how much he doesn't want to walk home with me.

It's dark outside. The street is full of kids; teenagers smoking, skateboarding, getting together money for party pills. All the other shops are shut and all the lights are off. There are three ways to walk home and probably four variations on each one of those ways. I take the 'stay close to shops as long as possible' way. It means I have something to look at most of the way home. It's cold. It feels like it's been dark all day. I leave for work in the dark. I leave for home in the dark. It's quite metropolitan, like living in London or New York, that's what Lee says. Lee has never lived in London or New York.

I can only stay close to the shops for so long and eventually I'm walking past workshops then houses and finally down our street, past the Playcentre Lyall and I went to, which is attached to the primary school we went to.

*

When I get home Lee and Nancy are around the dining table with their accountant and a real estate agent. Nancy looks up as I come in the door and says, 'Is that the time?' She looks at her watch. 'Lee, is that the time?' Lee looks at his watch and before long the accountant looks at his watch and the real estate agent all in escalating indignation: they're a Gilbert and Sullivan chorus. Nancy says, 'Lee, call Lyall and get him to drop off some takeaways on his way home. Get Lloyd a burger or something.' Lee gets his phone out of his pocket and I leave them looking at their watches some more and shaking their heads and go to my room. I take off my *Dollar Ninety-Five Store* T-shirt and listen to them talking about things. I crouch for a minute with my shirt off, looking through a drawer for something I want to wear. When I find a T-shirt I put it on and pull the drawer all the way out and kneel on the ground and reach my hand in. I pick the Sellotape off the back of the drawer and pull out the plastic bag of tranquilisers I've been saving up. In the the months I haven't been sleeping, in the dark I've been counting my teeth with my tongue and stroking the nail of my pointer finger with the pad of my thumb trying to catch my body working; exploring the machine of it, trying to be surprised.

As I stand up I see Lyall out my bedroom window. He's picking his way up the driveway in the dark carrying a bag of takeaways. He thinks no one can see him. It holds me, him walking and his face open like no one's watching. I move round and lean slightly out the window so I can watch him all the way to the door and just before he reaches the light of the house I say, 'Lyall,' not loudly, not like I expect him to hear, just like I'm naming something, a pen set, some lip gloss, an old friend. 'Lyall,' I say again and his head swings and he sees me and there's a second he's looking at me and still doesn't realise anyone's watching him – then it's gone and he raises his hand so he might be waving or he might be signalling stop but in that second, when he sees me without realising, the decision's made and I grab my wallet and my jacket and I stuff the pills in the pocket of my jeans and climb out of the window. Lyall looks worried as I walk over Nancy and Lee's lawn toward him. 'Lyall,' I say, 'Lyall, I'm going to have a beer. Come and have a drink with me.' It surprises neither of us. Lyall looks behind me and his face changes and it changes back. 'Lyall,' I say, 'I'm going to have a beer then I'm going to kill myself.' It feels like the time he takes when I remember that day; the same long, still moment. 'Lyall,' I say. 'Come on. It's my birthday.' Lyall laughs, it's not my birthday. 'One drink,' I say. Then it's quick. He looks at me and he puts the bag of takeaways on the lawn next to where he's standing and we walk into town.

We sit in the bar and drink and don't talk much and then I say, 'What do you call this?' I mean the waitresses in hula skirts and the torches and palm trees. Lyall looks around and shrugs and says, 'Tiki theme?' 'It's comfortable,' I say and drink some more. Lyall doesn't say anything. Neither of us say anything for a long time. Then Lyall says, 'How are you going to do it?' 'Pills,' I say. 'Pills and a plastic bag.' He nods and looks at his beer, then he wipes his mouth with his hand in a fist. 'I left,' he says. I smile and nod and, looking straight ahead of me, say 'You left.' I can feel him looking at me and I turn to look at him but he can't look at me and he turns away and his eyes flash like they're alive and he says, 'And I came back,' and I look away to give him some privacy and he says 'For you,' and I say, 'What?' and Lyall says, 'Nothing.' Then we sit in silence again. A waitress takes some bottles off our tables and leaves. 'I've got nothing for you Lloyd,' Lyall says, and he finishes his beer and reaches for his jacket. He gets up to leave and then he looks at me and leans down and it's his face in my hair and he says, just to me, 'Don't fuck up.' Then he puts his forehead to mine and I can smell the tears in his eyes like we're walking beside the sea together at night.

Over Again

It was Friday night. The city was busy and the bar was three deep. Lucy had been sitting at an outside table with Mark and Jane for most of the afternoon. Cyrus saw her on his way to the bar. He ordered a drink, came over, lit a cigarette and asked if he could join them. Lucy pushed her hair behind her ear. They drank some more. Talked about what brought Cyrus back from Melbourne and drank some more.

'How's Kate?' said Jane.

'Kate's great,' Cyrus smiled.

'We should get some dinner,' said Mark. 'Are you coming to get something to eat, Lucy?'

Lucy smiled and frowned at the same time, like she'd already eaten something she shouldn't have, and shook her head.

Mark and Jane left to get something to eat, shaking their heads.

'How much money do you have?' Cyrus said.

Lucy shrugged.

He said a friend of his was working at a bar and they could get more to drink. Lucy said, 'Sure.' They leaned on each other a little as they walked along the newly dark streets full of people shopping and going home. At the bar she paid for more drinks and they drank some more and shouted humid indignation in each other's ears. Cyrus said he had gin at his place and she said she had her car. Lucy drove in silence and at fifty-five, changing down at every corner, coming to a complete stop at every intersection.

In his bedroom she said she'd drunk enough, thinking about the drive home. She asked for a glass of water. He handed her a glass of gin and she said thanks. Her jaws were fluid and he was talking and playing music. It got later and she couldn't walk. Lucy thought, It's okay I don't need to walk to drive, and, I can't stay here, and, Don't stay here. Cyrus said, 'You could stay here.' Lucy said she needed to go to the bathroom. She climbed out the window and drove home, squinting and swearing and keeping all the street lights on one side.

The next day Lucy worked and every time the phone rang her stomach would lift and fall. Cyrus had her number – he had all her numbers. She left one client to throw up. One of the other nail technicians sent a trainee to see where she was. When the trainee knocked on the toilet door Lucy slid twenty dollars under it and told her to buy a small bottle of vodka, quickly. The afternoon went a lot quicker than the morning. One client offered her a breath mint and the rest fell into a parade of hands on towels. Hands attached to droning, underwater voices floating over her as she filed and stuck and painted in a cloud of acrylic. Her head swam for shore a little with every pull on her water bottle. She nodded and smiled and said not much. The last client left at half past five and Lucy stood with the trainee watching the till cash up. They drank the wine that was there for clients out of coffee mugs, swung in their chairs and talked about tonight. Lucy looked at the phone. As they pulled down the grille and locked it, the trainee said she should come out but Lucy said no, she was off for a quiet night.

On the way home, Lucy stopped at a supermarket and bought a lot of beer. The check-out person said, 'Quiet night at home?' She nodded and said, 'Uh-huh,' and, rubbing her face, looked down the long line of check-outs and people. At home she sat in her room and drank beer. Her flatmates came home, popped their heads around her door and left again. Two of them played some sort of robot game up and down the hallway with boxes on their heads and she laughed and said she needed to read some books. She thought she fell asleep with an ancient history textbook on her face.

Lucy woke up driving in silence and at fifty-five. There was a number written on her left hand in red ballpoint pen. The clock in her car said three thirty and her hand said *4*. Cyrus must have rung. It was dark and probably Sunday morning. She was heading for town with the street lights on one side. If she closed an eye she could probably make it.

She parked her car on a back street and looked around. There was half a bottle of whisky in her handbag which was on the seat beside her. Lucy drank some more, opened the door and got out. Even with one eye shut the key wouldn't find the lock, so she left it and wove her way toward the bar. She went upstairs and knocked on the closed door. No one answered. She knocked again and shouted and leaned against the door smiling until someone opened it. It was dark and loud and full of people.

The bartender said, 'Lucy! Thank God. I nearly go out of business every time you stop drinking,' and she laughed and he said, 'No. Really.' He leaned over the bar, touched her chin and said, 'Lucy. Come on. How about it?' She leaned back, pointed at him and looked around the room. She was still smiling.

While Lucy looked one way, a tap came from the other and Kate shouted, 'Thanks for coming.' Cyrus was beside Kate, in her arms. Arm in arm they stood there, in front of Lucy now that she'd turned round. He lifted his glass to her. 'Shall we discuss this outside?' said Kate. Lucy nodded, draining her drink.

They stood, the three of them, outside. Cyrus lit a cigarette and took a step out of Kate's way. Lucy lit a cigarette and Kate started. Basically, it was just everything she'd said on the phone. Lucy wasn't sure if she should run or nod politely. She looked at Cyrus for help and he gave her nothing and she looked at Kate still talking fast, something about her and something about him and something about Kate – and Melbourne, Cyrus working something out in Melbourne. The street fell away a bit from under her.

Could Lucy just see her way clear to do that? Kate stopped talking. No one was talking.

'Well, yeah,' said Lucy, 'of course.'

Kate had tears in her eyes. 'I wouldn't ask otherwise.'

'Yeah, sure, I totally understand.'

'I just think,' said Kate, 'we've got a chance this way. Cyrus and I.'

'Uh-huh,' said Lucy.

Kate hugged her. 'Thank you Lucy. I forgive you totally and set you free.'

Cyrus was smiling and not trying to hide it. Lucy could see it but Kate couldn't.

For a moment, Lucy saw how it would all turn out – in a month's time or a week's or tomorrow. Kate saying, 'You promised.' Lucy pretending she knew what that meant. Cyrus laughing behind Kate's back. Kate saying again, 'You need help, Lucy.' But this time Lucy punches her and, as Kate falls to the ground, strikes Cyrus across the face with something heavy and says, 'You can wipe that smile off too.'

Lucy woke up. Bright sunlight was cutting through a chink in the curtains – not her curtains. 'Fuck,' she said. She rolled onto her back – not her ceiling. 'Fuck,' she said more quietly. Cyrus slept. Kate wasn't there. It was fantastic – Lucy's life – like God had run out of things to happen to her and the same thing was happening over and over again and He was getting His inspiration from every stupid thing said about infidelity. Hopefully, it was Sunday, but running it through her head – the robot game, the conversation with Kate – there was no way it was

Sunday morning. It must be Monday, she needed to get to work. She got out of the bed and started collecting her clothes. Cyrus stirred and said, 'Where are you going?' without opening his eyes or lifting his head off the pillow. She didn't reply. Cyrus sat up and watched Lucy shake her head as she untangled her underwear and struggled to put them on.

'Come back to bed, Lucy. It's early.'

'I have to go to work.'

'Lucy, it's Wednesday.'

Lucy stopped dressing for a split second, then started again, hoping Cyrus hadn't seen her stop.

'Lucy, come back to bed.'

'Where's Kate?'

'Kate's dead.'

Lucy looked at Cyrus for the first time.

Cyrus ran his hand through his hair and looked away from Lucy. 'Lucy,' he said sternly and then started laughing. 'Fuck, okay, she's not dead. I wish she was dead – but she'll be at work by now, and she'll be there all day. Lucy, come back to bed.'

Lucy said 'Fuck' again under her breath. She pulled her T-shirt over her head and started looking for her skirt – Wednesday. It wasn't like she couldn't remember anything since the conversation on the street, it was just what she could remember felt like all part of one day, or an hour. It was an ordering problem not a loss problem. She picked her keys up off the floor.

'Your car's not here.' Cyrus was sitting against the wall behind the head of the bed. 'You might as well come back to bed. I carried you here over my shoulder. I went to your house and stole you from your bed while you were sleeping. You had nothing to do with it. I took complete advantage of you. Let me make you breakfast.'

They would have fired her by now. They'd probably fired her and hired someone to take her place if it was Wednesday. She put on her skirt. Cyrus was a prick, it was probably Sunday. Kate was probably on her way to take him out to brunch. Lucy couldn't find her shoes. She looked around the room.

'I told her not to call you,' said Cyrus. 'No, I begged her not to call you. I'm sorry you got dragged into it.'

Cyrus was a prick.

'It's not like she owns us,' Cyrus said. 'We're nothing to do with her.'

She couldn't find her shoes.

'Where are my shoes?' Lucy said.

'You weren't wearing them when you got here.'

She looked at her feet. She'd walked to his house in bare feet.

Someone who said they could help had written a phone number on the back of an EFTPOS receipt and handed it to her last winter in the lobby of the district court. The receipt was in the pocket of her warm jacket which was hanging on the back of the chair in her bedroom.

'Lucy, come back to bed.' Lucy looked from her feet to Cyrus. 'If you don't leave you won't have to keep coming back.' Nothing could help her. 'Lucy. Come on. She won't be back for hours.'

She picked up her sweatshirt from under the bed. She could call in sick. If it was Monday, she could call when she got home and say she was sick. It wasn't Wednesday.

She was due some good luck. In the whole economy of it she really was due some good luck. Her car was probably outside parked on the street with her shoes in it and it was Sunday, she could sleep the rest of the day and later on have a couple of wines with Jane and laugh about it. Kate wouldn't find out and the next she would hear from either of them would be a wedding invitation.

Lucy put her sunglasses on, Jesus Christ himself only knew why the fuck she had sunglasses and no shoes but she put them on like having them there was part of her plan from the beginning. Cyrus went to say something and she raised her hand to stop him. She felt bad and a fool and like this would go on for ever and ever. Everything there was to say had been said and promised and broken and said again, but she looked around the room one last time for something to say and there was nothing.

One of Your Skies

They say it started in your lungs. That's what your nephew tells me. Someone else tells me they can't tell where it started, just that it's everywhere now.

Your sister, Anne, asks what they're going to do. They say, realistically, you're not going to get better. She holds your hand. It's in your brain, that's why it hurts in your head. They've given you morphine and that's why it doesn't hurt now. They say you're not leaving the hospital. You know they mean alive. Anne took you to Accident and Emergency three weeks ago and they said it was viral. Your son, Benny, called Anne a week later saying he'd found you thrashing around. She came to stay. A couple of days ago you said you felt like fish. Anne cooked you some fish. You said you felt like curry sauce on your fish. She went out and bought curry sauce. When she got back you said you didn't feel hungry any more. This all comes out. They say you have options. You hear the word 'titrated' and think it sounds like bells. Your sister says it's for the best. You agree, sign some papers and they put in a drip.

You feel like a cigarette. When they ask if they can get you anything they don't mean cigarettes. By the afternoon, you can't move any more. Anne says she's just ducking out for a minute – for a cigarette. You try to ask her to get some patches while she's out but you can't move any more. You tried to give up once. You ended up wearing the patches and smoking at the same time and going to the doctor who said you were passing out because your heart was beating too fast. You've given up now.

Other people in the ward have their lunch. You've probably had your last lunch. The doctor explains to your sister that you're unconscious now and will just drift off. This is not a technical term. You're not thinking, I wish I spent more time working, and other clichés. You remember eating fish your son caught, and cockles you collected and opened over a fire by dark water alive with phosphorescence. It seems fitting but not altogether yours. You haven't seen your oldest son in a couple of months, maybe a year. Anne tells you she called him, he'll be here in a couple of days. So this drifting away, you think, and listen hard to see if anyone is mentioning time. You hurt. One at a time your insides expand, catch fire and start crawling around the dull ache that's everywhere. The pain starts to make noise and smell like sand. It's loud in your ears and the air around your face is warm and damp with it. You feel yourself drifting away from it and panic. Your sister's face may be the last one you see. You haven't seen yourself for days.

Anne's son says hello. You almost forget you can't move. Your sister's trying to be something her voice isn't. She asks her son to go to your house and get some of your spiritual books and find out where the hell Benny is. She tells him to stay here for a minute while she ducks out – for a cigarette. Her son sits down, then stands up, then tucks you in, then untucks you, then says nothing. The others wouldn't play with him. When it was his turn the other kids said they didn't want to play any more. He's the youngest, the tallest. Your sons look like small men next to him and they're not. He walks to the window, opens the curtains a bit and says, 'What about this weather?' and, 'The sky looks nice, Aunty Jo. It's one of your skies today.' You and he dig a hole and the warm water comes up. It gets hotter the closer you get to the sea, you tell him. The other kids are off somewhere with Anne. You say the hole is big enough but he keeps digging so you keep digging. You both jump in the sea to get cold first. The others come back and he hits his sister and your sons for no reason and says it's their fault. Anne comes back, tells him not to forget your books and to get Benny to call her when he finds him. She's got her mobile. Then it's you and her again like it has been for the last couple of months, since your mother died – old and confused.

You can't feel your eternal spirit self, if anyone's interested – hello? You can't feel your eternal spirit self. So don't start with don't forget the books. Forget the books. Forget Shakti Gawain, Kahlil Gibran, and *Conversations with God*. Find Benny and forget the books. Look in the middle of the road. That's where he was the other time he went missing, when he was four. In the middle of Panmure Drive, looking both ways like a dog off its lead. Your nephew should look there. That was the last place you looked. You checked all the closets. You checked under the car. You asked your oldest son over and over again; promising each time he wasn't going to get in trouble, you just needed to know. You checked under bushes, in the garage, in the boot of the car, behind the washing machine and upstairs. Then you decided to go for a walk and shout his name for a couple of blocks, 'Benny!' You bundled up your oldest son and when you got to the top of the driveway there he was, standing in the middle of peak hour traffic, counting. He looked worried but he said he wasn't. Your nephew should check there. That's where Benny went to think.

You could find him. If you had one more hour you could find him. Haven't you done enough for one more hour? You nursed your husband to death, you put your oldest son through flight school, and you gave regularly to charity. Surely that's enough for another hour. Any time now would be good. You could rise and walk again, leave this hospital, leave this bed and find Benny. You just needed an hour. It's not much to ask after everything you've done; an hour to say 'goodbye' and 'stop using drugs'. Why didn't you say that? In all the counselling and treatments, why did you say, 'I'm here,' and, 'Whatever you need'? Why didn't you say, 'Stop using drugs!' really loudly? Who would say that now? You need one more hour to tell someone to tell Benny to stop using drugs – loudly. Surely you've done enough for one more hour and any time would be good. Any time soon would be fine. Any time now would be good, or when your nephew brings him back. He should check the middle of the road, or the couch, or his bedroom where he keeps the curtains drawn and the stereo up – where he goes to think ever since he came home from Coolangatta. Ever since he came out of the psychosis he came home in from Coolangatta. Lots of sun in Coolangatta, people want to get away from the city, though. That's the mistake people make. People only visit the city but they really need to get away and go to the rivers: Nerang and that. Nerang's nice. It's a very spiritual place. Where are your books? What happens now and where the hell is your eternal spirit self? Any time now would be good.

Sleeping feels more like waking. You're padding round the ward in your bare feet, looking for a cup of tea. Waiting for the others to bring your clothes and take you home. You can't find your handbag, so you can't find your cigarettes, so you can't have a smoke. A nurse offers you a cigarette and you smoke it under a *No Smoking* sign on the mezzanine that looks out on the indoor garden. They have an indoor garden and you start to lift off the ground. Your feet lift off, toes last, and you take one more drag and throw the cigarette away as you fly over the indoor garden and leave it all behind and then there's a bang and you wake into darkness. More darkness and the pain's back and you scream and yell. Does no one know how much pain you're in and then there is no pain, as fast as that. You fly, like gliding, not swimming. You swoop and dive. The leaves from the trees flick when you pass them too close. You find your handbag in a high branch. You find your jeans and some underwear you haven't worn yet – you got them a month or so ago and they're still in their packaging. There's a little plastic pin holding the price tag on. You sit in the tree and pull the price tag and the pin stays so you use your teeth to break the pin, kissing the cotton, leaving lipstick on it. You can't remember putting on lipstick and you need a scarf because it was cold when you left. When you see a shoe you like, you buy two pairs – one in black and one in brown. If you had your handbag you could take yourself home, you could get takeaways on the way. It's nice to be hungry. You swing your feet and wait for your sister to bring the car round.

There are, it sounds like, ten maybe fifteen people in your room. Your oldest son is there, he sounds grown-up and he's not crying. He says, 'Yeah, I'm staying here.' Anne's here, and her son, and I'm here. There are some people telling your sister you will be free soon and does she mind if they pray? Anne says, 'Sure' but you say, 'Fuck off.' You won't help them get more time. You've done enough for one more hour. You've done more than them. And they say, 'God,' and any time now would be good. You don't see your sister leave the room and complain about the praying people and cry and call them bad names. When I find her she stops talking quickly and wipes her face and says she's popping out – for a cigarette. When you and I are alone, I tell you you're going on an adventure. I have no idea what to say. It's the only time I talk to you. I talk to both your sons and your nephew and try not to cry because it isn't worth anything now. I didn't want to come. People say, 'What's it all about?' and, 'It's sad,' and,

'She looks so peaceful'. Your sister keeps putting lipstick on you and people take turns putting water in your mouth with a sponge on a stick. No one else wants to leave at any time. I leave any time I can, to eat, to make phone calls, to have cups of tea with a friend who lives around the corner. I think about going to the museum to see the mammoth Anne used to call a flea-bitten old thing. On Sunday I leave and go home in an aeroplane. At the airport, Anne's husband says there was no real point in coming.

You notice I'm gone and then forget. You change your mind about it being for the best. You want one more hour. You try to tell your sister. It's like a bad dream, so you try to sleep. It's getting easier now. People keep you up sometimes, telling you things, like you're going on an adventure. Your mother comes, just to you, and knits but it doesn't make you feel calm. You would kill someone if it meant you could have one more hour. You would kill a child, a baby, an old person – someone else's baby – your own baby. You've been good enough for one more hour. If you killed someone, though, you'd want more than an hour, especially if it was Benny, you'd want – half again. That seems fair. Or you could go back – go to the doctor and find out you're sick and have treatment. Without this, that would be just as bad. That seems fair. You start to make lists about what you would be willing to do. You would kill those praying people – over and over. You have money. But you don't really care. It gets boring.

In a dream, maybe, you walk around the wards. You can't fly any more. You see children, sick and dying, and think you're Jesus. You place your hand on them and nothing happens. Your children bled a lot. Not more than anyone else probably, more likely the same. Your oldest son came home from Montana. He has a snow-kiting business there, it's successful. The dying children are just lying dying so you walk to the magazine shop. You never get time to read any more. Eternity's a long time, standing where you are now, flicking through magazines in your mind, on your deathbed.

Your sister opens the curtains and says, 'Good morning sweetheart.' It feels like a very important job you're doing; a factory job in a factory that makes important things for people. Time is fast. You're sad. You have no idea what you want. It's empty and hollow and nothing happens, over and over again. People fall into routine: meals, reading, visitors bringing food and soap. The room smells sick with flowers. You're sorry. Everyone said Benny might not live long. You wish everyone you loved was dead. Nothing anyone says is helpful. Dead people come and go – some of the children from down the hall, and none of it helps. The truth falls around you a little at a time, like deep water, but falling.

I call your sister most days and she holds the phone up to you and I have nothing to say except no. In my dreams you dream big, hopeful dreams and there is no romance or spiritual depth in any of it. No one arrives at anything that helps them. Everything you had and everything you lost and everything you kept safe is laid waste. I look for light and any dullness amounts to nothing. There is no useful problem, just days and days of end.

You die eventually and while I'm at work. Anne calls and says it's over. The woman who works opposite me is eating tuna from a can, a courier arrives and picks up a parcel for a company in town. My boss talks on the phone with his feet on his desk, looking out the window as a mist falls on the hills.

Everything

'How's Alex?' Hope said. She and Molly were sitting in a café by the river in early autumn drinking tea from the same pot. Molly sighed, looked out the window and said nothing.

'What?' Hope said.

Hope was Molly's friend and Alex was Molly's brother.

'How's Alex?' Molly said shaking her head and smiling.

'What?' Hope said, looking as surprised as she could.

Hope was married the first time she met Alex. He and Molly had been on the street tired from trying to buy a present for a family friend. 'There's Hope,' Molly said, waving. 'Let's have a coffee with Hope.' They were like a house on fire, Molly didn't miss it, couldn't miss it. Alex and Hope laughed, they smiled, they said, 'Oh, yeah, remember that' like old friends. Three months after Hope's husband left, Molly suggested afternoon tea at a café in the gardens. It was a warm day. Hope arrived first. Molly and Alex arrived together. That was a year ago.

'What?' Hope asked again.

'I did everything I could,' Molly said. 'This close,' she pinched her fingers together for effect.

'He liked the artist,' said Hope.

'"He liked the artist",' Molly mocked. 'He liked you.'

Hope felt surprised for real. She looked at Molly and didn't say anything.

'Don't blame me – or the artist. You two did it,' Molly pointed from Hope to an imaginary Alex then back again a couple of times. 'We sat in that café and you said, "I'm happy," and he said, "I'm happy alone, too," and then you said, just to make sure it was good and dead, "I'm just not ready for a relationship at the moment."'

Hope tried to remember. That wasn't the last thing they'd said. They'd talked for another hour after that and gone for a walk and talked some more. She'd thought it went well. Then two weeks later he'd started going out with a woman who was an artist.

'I just thought he didn't like me,' said Hope, only meaning to think it, but saying it out loud.

'And that,' said Molly, 'is what chokes it before it starts. You think he doesn't like you, then he thinks you don't like him and neither of you want to look like you like someone who doesn't like you, then before you know it he's going out with the artist, who's as dull as ditchwater, and you're alone and asking me, "How's Alex?", hoping beyond hope he's single again but if he was it wouldn't make a blind bit of difference because you and Alex would be so wary that eventually one of you would say something and it would all be off again.'

'He doesn't like the artist?' Hope said.

'He loves the artist,' Molly said. 'He's happy. That's not my point.'

'It all worked out fine then,' Hope offered, playing with a teaspoon that was lying on the table.

'It looks that way,' said Molly and then she said nothing for a moment, hoping it would sink in – how no one should settle for fine, how they'd both be much happier if they hadn't said what they'd said; if they'd just said what they felt and not been so worried about things working out fine. Then she asked how work was.

'Work's work – you know,' said Hope.

Molly knew.

'It's busy,' Hope added. 'What about you?'

Molly said the wedding would be in January. She would be baptised in December and Ned would marry her in January.

'I'll grow my hair,' said Molly.

'Summer wedding,' said Hope.

The wedding invitation – Hope's invitation – she returned with 'and partner' struck out. Molly counselled bringing someone.

'Anyone?' Hope said.

Molly saw her dilemma.

They met for an early dinner in spring and ate hot soup with noodles. As Molly put on her jacket she said she had to meet her fiancé. Hope laughed and said, 'That sounds flash,' and Molly laughed too.

Hope walked home along the river, like an actor in an eighties music video for a New Wave song about leaving. The sun had no heat in it and the ducks made her cold.

Molly lived by the beach and swam most days. She said dinner would be around seven but Hope could come any time after work. Alex and his artist were coming too – was that all right?

'Of course,' Hope said, like Molly couldn't imagine how all right it was. Like nothing had ever been so all right before.

'I'll see you after work,' Hope said.

At work things went badly. The salon was busy. The manager said 'Stop running' to anyone who was. She asked if Hope could keep an eye on the running while she went to lunch.

'It's supposed to be a relaxing place,' the manager said.

A woman handed Hope a page ripped from *Hustler* magazine. Hope folded it so only the head of the woman was showing, not the motorcycles or the men or her breasts. The woman wanted to be blonde – *Hustler* magazine blonde. Hope had three clients waiting, all with wet hair. An hour later the person doing the *Hustler* colour asked Hope to check it and as they walked over whispered something about 'very hot' and 'metallic dye'. They rinsed the woman's hair and it came out in *Hustler*-blonde jelly clumps. The manager came over to ask if anyone had been running and looked in the basin and looked at Hope and Hope looked at the jelly blocking the plug hole in the basin. She asked someone to put a conditioning treatment on the woman's hair for fifteen minutes.

Hope walked through the mall to the staff toilet and threw up, and prayed, 'God, if you get me out of this one I'll do anything – anything.' When she got back to the salon the woman's boyfriend was there. He was huge and wearing a gang patch.

'For some reason,' Hope said, 'it hasn't taken. We'll need to do the colour again. We won't charge you for it.' She would get herself out of it.

By six o'clock everyone had left the salon except the woman, her boyfriend and Hope. He swivelled oversized in a chair reading *Woman's Day* to them both. By seven o'clock Hope had put up what was left of the women's hair like a southern belle and she and her boyfriend left smiling.

Hope saw every side of herself in mirror after mirror after mirror as she cleaned up. She washed her hair leaning over a basin and dried it with the music turned off.

That was why it was late and dark when Hope got to Molly's house. She walked up the path, overgrown with seagrass and flax. She walked across the lawn in the noise of the coast under a full moon in a clear sky and knocked on the glass of the French doors. Molly shouted, 'Come in,' and opened the door.

Alex's girlfriend was at a yoga retreat and Molly's fiancé had been called in to work.

'That sounds flash,' Hope said.

'Make yourself at home,' Molly said.

As Hope entered the lounge, walled with books and

art, Alex stood up. She took a seat as far away from him as possible in the small dully-lit room.

'I'm just finishing dinner,' Molly said as she walked back to the kitchen.

'We waited for you,' Alex said, not in a cruel way. 'Shall I take your coat?'

'Oh yes,' Molly shouted from the kitchen. 'For God's sake Sasha, take her coat.'

They stood as in a queue and Alex's hand touched Hope's arm as he took her coat.

'She'll wear it all night otherwise,' Molly said, passing Alex in the doorway, 'so she can make a quick getaway.' She carried fresh bread and shouted for Alex to bring the pasta on his way back.

Molly said grace.

'Isn't this dreadful?' Alex asked Hope, throwing a thumb at Molly to indicate he meant the praying.

Molly hit him playfully, still praying with her eyes closed and head down.

'Honestly,' Alex said, 'don't you think this is dreadful?'

'You're the one breaking bread,' Hope said.

'Converted for a man,' Alex said.

'Jesus,' Hope said. Alex didn't mean Jesus.

'She won't watch Almodóvar any more,' he said.

'Probably for the best,' Hope said and they all laughed.

'Dig in,' Molly said.

Hope told them about the jelly clumps and the gang patch and the pornographic picture and said, 'I prayed.'

'No atheists in foxholes,' Alex said and they all laughed. They laughed like they used to laugh together before the engagement and the afternoon tea. Like the teacher was out of the classroom and the cat was away.

When the meal was finished they drank, still sitting at the dining table, and shouted about politics like someone, other than them, was listening.

'God will look after it,' Molly said.

'You don't really believe that, do you?' Alex said.

'God will look after it one way or the other,' Molly said, 'and for now I'm acting as if I believe that.'

'You realise how stupid that sounds?' Alex said. 'Hope, tell her how stupid it sounds?'

Hope agreed, perhaps because of the wine, that it did, indeed, sound stupid.

'No stupider than sitting here shouting about it,' Molly said and laughed and it was made light of again.

They tiptoed at it all night: the wedding, the conversion for the wedding, what she was wearing to the wedding. Just for the sport of it; an exercise in wit-sharpening, like some contest of the privileged classes. No one was trying to change anyone else's mind – not really.

The seats at the table got uncomfortable and Alex looked at his watch and something broke a bit in the spirit of it all.

'When does she get back?' said Hope, as if to make sure it was good and broken. So no one thought she was trying to fix it.

'Tomorrow,' said Alex, 'later in the afternoon.'

'Mmm,' said Molly and began to clear the table.

'What's that supposed to mean?' Alex said.

'What?' said Molly.

Hope stood up, took Alex's plate and said, 'How close is the retreat?'

'About an hour's drive,' Alex said. 'She caught a bus. I'll pick her up, later in the afternoon – tomorrow.'

Hope nodded and looked at her watch so it looked like it didn't matter to her and she was just making conversation.

Molly came back into the room with a new bottle of wine and said, 'Wine?'

Hope looked at Alex and Alex looked at Hope like actors in a Mexican standoff.

Molly said, 'For fuck's sake, come and have some more wine. Everything's not everything – it's just a glass of wine.'

Alex and Hope laughed.

'Well, Jesus,' Molly said walking unsteadily into the lounge, 'you never do anything – either of you. You always think everything's everything.' She struggled with the wine bottle and the corkscrew then handed them to Alex. 'You're always like "Oh. Oh. What if this is everything? I better sit here in complete stasis until I find out if it's everything. Oh, there it goes. It wasn't."'

Alex poured the wine. 'I'll tell you one thing,' he said, 'I'm glad religion is giving you such clarity and articulation.'

Molly threw a cushion at him and they both laughed.

Hope leaned in the doorway and watched them.

'Stop looking poignant and come and have a drink,' Molly said to her and she joined them in the lounge.

They drank and talked. Molly said she believed she

was doing the right thing. Alex and Hope said they supported her fully. Molly cried a little and Hope hugged her. Alex said he was only joking before. Hope said, slurring a little, 'If you do this, you can be sure of your afterlife.' Alex wasn't sure how saying that helped. Hope said, 'On the up side.' Molly nodded and drank more wine. Alex put on some music and they talked some more and laughed some more and forgot about everything.

The wine ran out and the music stopped and they sat in silence for a while. Molly made a snuffling noise, curled up beside Alex on the couch.

Hope said, 'Is she faking?'

Alex poked Molly. She repositioned herself and stayed asleep.

'She's faking,' Hope said. 'Molly. Molly.'

Molly stayed asleep.

'Don't wake her up,' Alex said.

'She's not asleep,' Hope said. 'She's faking.' Hope stood up to shake Molly. Alex caught Hope's arm and said, 'Don't wake her up.'

The house was quiet.

'We could go somewhere,' Alex said.

A key turned in the lock and the door opened. Alex let Hope's arm go. Molly stirred and woke. Ned came into the lounge and said, 'Hi Alex – Hope.' He kissed Molly on the head, and she stretched.

'I'm going to get a coffee.' Ned took off his coat. 'Does anyone want a coffee?'

'I'll help,' Hope said and followed him into the kitchen

where he sat on a stool and she made coffee. She asked how his night had been and he sighed by way of a reply.

'How about yours?' he said.

Hope shrugged then nodded and said, 'Yeah. Good.'

'Where's Alba?' Ned asked.

'Yoga retreat,' Hope said. 'She gets back tomorrow. Alex is picking her up later in the afternoon.' She straightened the tea towel that was hanging on the oven handle.

When she came back into the lounge, Alex was gone. She tried to hide the fourth mug; ashamed of it – of herself. Like she and the mug were the only things in the world. Hope drank her coffee fast and it burned everything in her mouth – tongue, cheek, gums. She looked at her watch. It was the tilt forward that did it. Hope said, 'I better go,' looking up to hold the large tears where they were, to stop them from tipping.

Molly said, 'Oh Hopie – stay.'

'No,' Hope said.

Molly saw Hope to the door and they hugged. Hope stood back and wiped her eyes as if she was tired, and looked at the wall behind Molly.

'You two,' Molly said – or, 'You too,' Hope wasn't sure.

'Your coat!' Molly went to get it.

Hope walked across the lawn in the sound of the night and the moon. As she drove home, she thought maybe Molly had said 'You to . . .' like she was telling Hope where to go – to make everything all right – but it was late now and it made no sense – none of it.

When You're Sick

She liked to imagine herself places. A small coastal cottage on the way out to the albatross colony, perhaps Otakou, with the fire going and some soup on the stove and people on their way, or perhaps already there – staying over. People visited her wherever she imagined she was. Unexpected people – Henry James, her aunt, the Tudors – mostly dead people and ones she wanted to have sex with, or had stopped having sex with after things went cold, usually through her fault.

Or Portland, Oregon on a spring day with snow still on Mount Hood – the Clearing. She made new friends in Portland. Portland was alive with possibilities, jobs she'd never heard of, halls full of red and orange food, sweating with beta-carotene and antioxidant. She would see the world from a different angle in Portland, go to some sort of department store and buy toxin-free, fair-trade sneakers made entirely from old tyres.

On Friday she went to a gallery opening, the launch of a video installation. She looked around and thought, 'This could be Portland.' She looked and tried not to listen and soaked it all in, the feeling of being in Portland in her new sneakers. Michael said, 'Sally – you look well.' She wanted to shout, 'Portland, Portland, Portland – they call it the Clearing, don't you know?' As she walked home she imagined her feet on Portland footpaths, going past Ankeny, Burnside, Davis and Flanders until she lost herself in the chatter of it all – the Willamette and the Columbia rushing by, or perhaps quietly, hardly even moving. She wasn't sure what rivers that size did.

On Saturday she went to the acupuncturist. The acupuncturist said, 'Honey, you don't want to go to Portland when you're sick – bad energy in Portland.' She showed her a book that explained why she had eleven needles in each of her ankles and why she needed to surround herself in positive light. The acupuncturist gave her an envelope with a postcard in it and said, 'This is for you to think about.' It was a postcard of Claremont – the city of trees. She imagined herself underwater – sleeping on a bed of bull kelp. Everything was exactly the right temperature. When she moved her arm, or her head, or pushed her hair behind her ears, the whole ocean – all of it – moved to adjust things so she stayed completely comfortable; every part of her supported and held by the perfectly temperate waters. There were no fish but the people who visited could breathe there, like her. She left the postcard, back in its envelope, for the next person to think about.

On Sunday she breaks the surface of the water in

Landmannalaugar, with the Northern Lights spread out above her. She leans back and lets them take her breath away. 'It's beautiful,' Michael says.

'It's ridiculous how beautiful it is,' she says.

Iceland had never occurred to her.

Like a Good Idea

It was a sunny day. The receptionist gave Polly a form to fill out and said she would get a nurse. She came back carrying a Polaroid camera and said, 'Can you stand by that wall?' Polly stood by the wall and the receptionist took the photo. She shook the photo for a minute, said Polly could sit down and walked away. A nurse came and took the form off Polly and told her, 'Follow me.' They went into a small room with a high window. Polly could see the top branches of a magnolia in flower outside. The nurse looked at the form.

'It says here you've been thinking about killing yourself,' the nurse said. 'When did you last think about killing yourself?'

'An hour ago?' Polly said.

The nurse wrote something. 'It's not okay to think about killing yourself. Thinking about killing yourself is not okay. Understand?' Polly nodded. 'If you think about killing yourself while you're here you need to tell someone. Understand?' Polly nodded. 'Understand?'

'Yeah,' Polly said. This all seemed like a very bad idea right now.

The nurse turned the form over. 'It says here you haven't had a drink or drug for a month. It's important that's the truth. If you go into detox you could die, so it's important that's the truth. Do you understand what the truth is?' Polly nodded. 'Is it the truth that you haven't had a drink or a drug for a month?' Polly shook her head. 'How long has it been since you had a drink or a drug?' Polly looked at her watch. 'I see,' said the nurse and wrote something down. 'We need to look in your suitcase now.'

Polly opened up her suitcase on the examination bed in the small room. The nurse took her perfume, her hairspray, her vitamin C tablets, her paracetamol and the small amount of vodka she had hidden in a toner bottle. 'If you get a headache, tell a nurse,' she said. 'If you get a cold, tell a nurse. You won't need hairspray here.'

The nurse wrote some more on the form then took out a laminated sheet of paper with writing on it. 'These are the rules of this drug treatment facility. You need to read them.' Polly picked up the laminated sheet, looked at it and put it on the desk. The nurse finished writing, put down her pen and looked at Polly. 'Have you read the rules of this treatment facility?' Polly nodded. The nurse pointed at the sheet. 'If you drink you'll be discharged. If you take any drugs not given to you by a member of medical staff, you'll be discharged. If you form an emotional or physical bond with another patient which is deemed inappropriate by a member of therapeutic or medical staff you will be discharged. If you start a fight, start a fire, disobey – do you get the picture?' Polly nodded. 'There's no pressure to sign this form.' The nurse pushed another form towards Polly. 'By signing this form you're admitting yourself. You can turn around and leave right now. There are twenty other people who want your bed. I'm a taxpayer, so if you're wasting my money don't sign the form.' Polly signed the form, mainly to prove something to the nurse.

'You can have cups, not bottles. You're not allowed to have water bottles.' Lorna was Polly's buddy. They were going to be in the same therapy group. She was a middle-aged woman, wearing track-pants and slippers. They both wore name tags. 'There's a lot to take in on your first day.' When they got back to the dormitory, Lorna said, quietly, 'Do you think you'll be hanging out?'

'Oh, no.' Polly shook her head and stuck her hands in her pocket.

'It's just, if you are, you should probably tell a nurse.'

Polly nodded.

'You're in now. That stuff about being one month clean – they don't really mean it once you're in.'

A group of about ten women arrived in the dormitory, shouting and laughing.

'You'll have your own room soon, anyway.' Lorna left.

The next morning Polly went to Occupational Therapy. The nurse told her she could paint a scarf or make a belt. Polly said she didn't care which and the nurse said she needed to start caring around about now, and did she realise where she was? Polly said nothing and the nurse said, 'You're in a mental institution, an asylum, because of the choices you've made. I'm giving you a choice. Right now is where you need to start caring about the choices you make.' She had a silk scarf in one hand and a length of leather in the other. She was holding them up like they were two fish she was about to win a prize for. 'Do you want to make a belt or a scarf?'

'I really want to make a belt,' Polly said.

'So there's no one in the world you could give a scarf to?'

'I could make a scarf for my grandmother.'

'That's the spirit,' the nurse handed her the scarf. 'Thinking of others is always the right choice.'

An hour later the nurse came over to the table Polly was working at. It was beside the window and the sun was streaming in.

'Are those poppies?' she said to Polly. 'You can't draw poppies. I think I explained that.' Polly turned the flowers into balloons. They looked awful but the nurse said they were much better and she needed to get used to not being such a perfectionist. The scarf really did look awful – like a five-year-old had made it. Her grandmother was dead so it didn't bother Polly.

She wasn't ready to tell anybody but when the judge had said she could have prison or treatment, treatment seemed like a good idea. It was testing her, though. It was like prison but with smiling nodding people sweating earnestness, every moment of every day: psychotherapy, meditation, interpretive dance. She'd been there three days and was already carrying round a stuffed blue bear. She'd been to grief group, and the facilitator, a large woman wearing peach, had said Polly needed to look after her inner child, since she seemed to hate her inner child, and she'd given Polly the bear. If Polly was seen without it or damaging it in any way by any of the staff she would be discharged, and if she was discharged the sentence would stand and she would go to prison. As she sat in the big dining hall, eating lasagne with the bear on its own chair, she wondered if prison might have been the better option. She had to write her life story up until today and read it to her group tomorrow.

She'd come from a good home. She'd gone to a good school then she'd gone off the rails. She didn't know if she could stop because she'd never tried to stop. They sat in a room with no windows, in a circle, ten of them and the counsellor, Bill. She'd fleshed it out a little, but it boiled down to that. Bill wasn't convinced. He asked if she was convinced. Polly said quickly, 'Yeah, sure, I can see it all now.' Bill said again that he wasn't convinced and asked if anyone else in group wasn't convinced. People started mumbling that they weren't sure.

'You don't sound very remorseful,' one of them said finally.

If they'd wanted remorse she could have done remorse. She hadn't wanted to lay it on too thick. The counsellor suggested Polly write a letter to her mother and ask how her drug use had affected her family. Polly said she wasn't allowed to contact her mother so that probably wouldn't work. The counsellor said he would contact Polly's mother and ask her to send a letter explaining how Polly's drug use had affected her family.

'I don't think that's really necessary,' Polly said.

No one talked for what seemed like a long time.

'Well,' said Bill, 'if you don't think it's necessary Polly, I think it's absolutely imperative that I do it today.' He turned to another new woman and asked her to read her life story.

'I was born into an alcoholic family,' she began. 'I never wanted to turn out like my parents.' She began to cry. 'I was molested when I was three years old and that's when I stopped feeling.'

'I would really prefer it if you didn't contact my mother.' Bill and everyone else in group turned toward Polly, while the other new woman cried in quiet chokes.

'Polly,' said Bill, 'we're listening to Rebecca's story.'

'I know, and I'm sorry, but I would really prefer it if you didn't contact my mother.' Polly was folding and unfolding the piece of paper she'd written her life story on. 'Maybe I can rewrite this tonight and present it again tomorrow.'

'Where's your bear, Polly?'

Polly looked around the legs of her chair.

'Fuck.' She'd left the bear in her room. 'I mean – flip!'

'Does anyone else find it interesting that Polly has lost her bear?' Bill asked the group. No one answered. 'What do you think it says to me about you that you've lost your bear, Polly?'

Polly shrugged. It was hopeless.

'Rebecca,' Bill said, 'what does it say to you about

Polly that she loses her bear and then interrupts you at your most vulnerable?'

'Umm.' Rebecca grabbed a tissue from the box on the table in the middle of the circle. 'I don't think it shows much concern for me – or her.'

'What do you think of that, Polly?'

If she left now, she could be in Christchurch within a couple, maybe three, hours. If she was smart about it, she would leave after group. It was free time. No one would miss her until dinner and that would give her a head start. She could score by nightfall. The police were busy, too busy to worry about her for a couple of days. She could get a couple of days out of it, surely.

'And if you stay you could get a lifetime of freedom.' Polly looked at Bill. It was a lucky guess. She could take him. It was a lucky guess. He was small and weak and stupid. There was no way he would fight back. There was probably something in his contract that said he couldn't fight back. He was an idiot. Not even that lucky – she doubted there was anyone in the room who wasn't thinking about leaving. He liked to tell people what to do, that was clear: he liked to be right. He was a very small man. The smallest in the room. If she started it, there were at least five in the group who would join in.

'You really want another assault charge?' Bill said. Polly knew it was a trick, like this whole stinking place. She shook her head.

'I'm sorry for interrupting, Rebecca,' Polly said, and Rebecca carried on.

*

Polly sat on a balcony outside the nurses' station smoking a cigarette and watching a game of touch rugby. More than one staff member said, 'You could join in' as they walked past her. Crying was the key. They were trying to break everyone, and crying was the key. Bill would ring her mother, her mother would write a letter and when he read it out she needed to cry. Rebecca had cried. It was the opposite of anywhere else Polly had been. In some ways it was worse. They wanted you to do certain things and the easiest way through was to pretend to do those things. She'd done that for years. She'd just got off to a bad start because it was different here. She'd be fine now.

'You're shaking.' It was Bill.

Polly threw her cigarette into a sand-filled ice cream container and folded her arms.

'Have you seen the nurse about that shaking?'

Polly nodded.

'Polly, do you have any idea about the truth?' It was like a nightmare of compassion.

'I saw the nurse yesterday, is what I meant.'

'Okay, were you shaking yesterday?'

'No, but I figured you were just talking in general, had I seen the nurse kind of thing. Sorry.'

'You can't con a con, Polly.'

'Is *28 Days* like your favourite Sandra Bullock movie, or do you and your boyfriends sit around watching all of them?' She hadn't meant to say it. She hadn't meant to say it then, anyway. From Bill's immediate reaction she wasn't even sure she had said it. She'd been hoping to save it for later; the end, where she throws her chair and storms out and goes to prison and tells them all to fuck themselves and scores.

'I wish I could show you what it's like, Polly. Just for five minutes, I wish I could take my life and give it to you, just for five minutes. You have no idea what you're about to miss.' For a split second she wanted it. Then it was gone.

A Lightness

They were on the top of the slide when it happened. He pushed her and she fell and as she hit the ground all the life punched out of her. It was three days before Christmas and they were two years old.

He didn't remember it. His mother said she arrived at Playcentre late because she'd been shopping and his father had walked to the fence to meet her. His father said he said, 'Your son has been very violent this afternoon,' then his mother's face went, 'Oh.' His father turned to see what she was looking at and the girl was on the ground dead. They said Mickey was leaning over the top of the slide looking at her, that when he saw his parents looking he smiled and waved. He slid down the slide and ran to the swings. The girl's mother saw Mickey push her. Earlier he'd pushed another child's head into the corner of a table. The week before he'd gone up to several children and grabbed them in what parents thought was a hug, then, with all his weight, dropped them to the ground. When he thought about it now, he couldn't imagine what could have made him that angry.

He didn't think about it now, not much. His grandmother had lived in a council flat at the time. He would stay with her while his parents were in the business of apologising and wondering. They'd waited a long time to have a child; his grandmother was old and slightly disappointed. He had memories of being in her flat; the warmth that hung there and expanded inside him. He remembered wine biscuits and orange cordial. In the sobbing days after his father left, Mickey's mother said his grandmother blamed her completely. The fruit doesn't fall far from the tree. When his mother got older and went swimming every day and to the church hall on Wednesday mornings for yoga she said that, once, on the way to Playcentre, Mickey had asked if the dead girl would be there. She said it while she was doing dishes one cold night, out of the blue and unprompted; jazz was playing. In his mind there had always been a pop. He supposed it was the small girl's kidneys or her heart.

Mickey became his own man. His father invited him to the beach life he led with a young woman he had met through sailing. His mother was happy for Mickey to go for a couple of weeks. She'd moved to a smaller house with a larger garden where she grew organically. She cooked high-smelling mixtures that swamped the house and stung high into Mickey's sinuses whenever he came in from the air. He went to a private boys' high school. As he was leaving to catch the bus that would take him to the train that would take him to his father she ran after him waving a small brown glass bottle. 'Valerian,' she said, handing it to him, 'for sleeping.' She looked him in the eye. His father paid for the school. Paid highly for the beach life he was having. He would call it a waste. In the office, after the principal said, 'We have no choice but expulsion,' and he never paid for anything again. Mickey's mother organised him into the local high school and said, 'It'll all be for the best.'

It was 1995. Mickey wore tapered jeans, tidy shoes and a fishtail parka. He worked as a painter in the school holidays and didn't smoke. He was quiet and studious, intelligent and well presented. He met up with a friend from primary school called Davey and they became close again. On Friday nights he would take the bus into town, shop for new clothes, meet his dealer in a café and after a few beers in the public bar of a hotel go to the bathroom and take a handful of amphetamines. They would get to the club around midnight and everyone would be there. Mickey would dance and around five he, Davey and a few others would wander back to Davey's house and play music until midday when the others would fall one by one into heavy sleep. Mickey and Davey would stay up and talk and play more records and sometimes draw maps of things, grinding their teeth. The others would wake and go home. As they left Mickey and Davey would try to involve them in complex, fast-talking, nose-wiping conversations to which the others would, one by one, shake their heads and leave. When all of them were gone, Mickey would say, 'Beer?' and he and Davey would start drinking. Sometimes, on late winter afternoons, Davey's mother would come to the door of Davey's bedroom and say, 'Are you here for dinner, Mickey?' They weren't hungry but they sat at the dinner table and talked with Davey's father and mother and Davey's older brother. Sometimes Davey's mother would say, 'Your mother called.' Their mothers had been on the PTA of the primary school together and hadn't rekindled a friendship. Mickey would bite his nails. It would start as grooming: he would feel the snag of a loose nail and try to flatten it and before he knew it his nails were down to the quick on both hands, then he'd start on the skin around his nails. He would twitch, both he and Davey would twitch at dinner and look at things that weren't always there. They were never hungry and at about ten they would get a phone call and someone might come and pick them up and they would go out again. More pills, more drinking and perhaps they would watch the sun come up from the port, or the top of a hill, or sitting on a bench in the park beside the university. It was like this a lot. Almost always, but the details were different. Different combinations of friends that joined them in Davey's bedroom, different music, different cars, bikes, different meals, different drinks, different weather, it would rain sometimes, sometimes the dawn would swelter rather than break. There were always new clothes, shoes, haircuts. Generally though, if someone wanted to find him, that was where Mickey would be – with Davey.

He'd been with Davey the night she said it happened, at least that's what they told everyone. She said Mickey had raped her in an alleyway behind the club. Mickey told the police he didn't even like her. She withdrew her complaint. His mother said it seemed that Mickey didn't seem to understand how serious the allegations were. He said she didn't seem to believe her own son. She said he had a power of anger in him and he told her to fuck herself and went to Davey's crying most of the way and sucking back pills. He started smoking. Davey's mother knocked on the door every couple of hours and asked if Davey was sure Mickey wasn't in there. Davey said he hadn't seen Mickey and she said she didn't want him hanging round him any more. Davey begged his brother for sleeping pills and Mickey fell asleep on Davey's bedroom floor under his fishtail parka. Mickey dreamed, vivid and clear; there was a boy on top of the slide as well as the small girl. He let the boy slide down before he pushed the girl off fucking her all the way to the ground where she popped her sickening pop and he couldn't wake up until the morning, when Davey shook him. They walked out of the house together, with Davey's mother shouting at Davey that Mickey needed to go and Davey needed to stay. Davey told her to fuck herself and she shouted louder and louder and higher and higher as they walked down the driveway. Davey's father read the paper.

They spent the early morning walking, talking, not trying to piece the night back together so much as working out where they would go from here. It would go silent now and then until Mickey said, 'I don't even like girls.' Davey nodded and although Mickey couldn't see him nod he knew he was nodding. They stopped walking at the park beside the university and sat on a bench in front of a fountain. They sat and Mickey cried silently, then shaking. Davey held him and watched the fountain and couldn't help thinking how fucked everything was and how unfair and how fucked it was going to be from now on, and complicated.

She was pregnant. Mickey was waiting for the bus one day after school; he'd waited in the library until everyone else was gone. He saw her crossing the road toward him and he almost threw up with fear. She stood in front of him in the bus shelter and asked if she could sit next to him. He looked up and didn't say yes. She sat down beside him. 'I'm pregnant,' she said. He said he didn't believe her and she said it was him and handed him a piece of paper which he didn't look at, which he never looked at. 'I think we could make it work,' she said. 'Do you want to go for a walk?' He told her to fuck herself and she said she would press charges. He said she had to be joking and she said she wasn't joking. She said he bit her and she was still missing a piece of her shoulder and she showed him. He looked behind her – for Davey. Did he want to see if the bit missing fitted the shape of his mouth? She was sure it did. She was sure somehow, somewhere, someone could probably prove it was him who had bitten the piece out of her shoulder, a dentist perhaps. He said he would go to the police. She said, 'They can tell who children's fathers are.'

Despite everything, he enjoyed her company. Davey said he should move to Australia. Mickey said maybe things would turn out okay. Maybe it was one of those funny stories people tell about how they got together. Davey said, because no one else would, 'These are the funny stories: either you consensually fucked her in an alley and she falsely accused you of rape, or you didn't fuck her at all and she got someone else to fuck her in an alleyway and bite a chunk out of her shoulder.' Mickey said it wasn't like that. Davey said, 'Or you raped her in a blackout and she still wants to go out with you.' Mickey looked at Davey for the last time. 'Fuck you,' Mickey said, 'fuck you, you fucking fag,' and walked away.

She never got any bigger and she never had a baby and Mickey never asked. He was in a deep hole now, he did what she said because he was scared – scared of what she'd do, scared of what he'd done, and sad, a private heartbroken sickness, it was the only thing that was his, everything else was hers because of what he'd done. At night while she slept he would fit his teeth around the hole in her shoulder and think about that piece of her body inside him. He would get out of bed, go to their bathroom and cut small pieces out of his body with a knife he hid for the purpose. He would turn the pieces over in his hand in the cool glow his eyes made in the night. She was funny and intelligent and she thought the world of him. They finished university and got married, they travelled, they came home and had their first child when they were both twenty-five. Then they had another, and another and then she said he was having an affair and they broke up. He moved to a three-bedroom house in the Waitakeres thinking he would need room for his children. She fought him for custody and brought up the scar on her shoulder and the record of the report of the rape and he was offered supervised visits and declined them. His mother said 'Convenient'; she said he never took responsibility for anything and he agreed and picked up the bill for the lunch they'd shared at a café near the family court. He kept working and lived in the large house in the bush; he was thirty-eight. His mother got older and meaner and stopped tending her garden. He never heard from his father.

He had more than enough time to look at his life to this moment. There wasn't a part of him that didn't doubt what a waste he had made of it. He never blamed luck or fate, he just looked back and thought, this is the story, I made this, I am this. Sometimes he thought about Davey with some hope, somehow maybe that was the glue he needed to find but then he phoned him and Davey didn't return his call. He looked at himself and saw he hated women, he was frightened of what he did to women. What people told him he did to women. He had been a good father. When his own children were small he had been gentle and kind. She had yelled a lot and shouted and shifted the children with immense force and he had been kind and gentle, hadn't he been kind and gentle? No, she said, and the court agreed. He had raped her. He became more and more sure of it, and he'd killed that small girl. With his hate and his brute force, he'd killed her, he'd thrown her off the slide. He'd thought about it for a long time before he did it, it was calculated and cruel. This is how he moved in the world, working hard at his job, because everything was empty including the job but it had a time sheet and he could fill out the little fifteen-minute blocks with what he did in his day and that seemed like a way to move through life.

Then one night, not a darker night than any other, not lighter, he sat in a comfortable chair and ran it over in his head one more time. Everything he'd killed or been complicit in the killing of was in his house now.

The air was thick with microscopic things: the measles virus, encephalitis, tuberculosis. Small winged insects he injured mortally going about his everyday business. A few he'd slapped on his arms and legs while at the beach or picnics. Larger flies and cockroaches patrolling the higher surfaces for crumbs and flakes. Then birds, sitting on the sills and bookcases, caught under his car or flung against the windows of his house. A house that would not have been there if it wasn't for him. Poisoned mice, rats and possums shuffled and fought with each other both in his sight and under things so he could only hear them. Family pets – put down, run over, crawled away to die – now wiped themselves on his legs and purred. And the food ones, lambs, cows, chickens, the monkey he'd eaten in Thailand, the horse he'd eaten in France, some of the cats he didn't altogether recognise. Pot plants left to flounder. Then, more abstractly, rabbits from Draize tests. Silkworms. The long extinct and almost extinct because of the constant tramp forward of the human race. Fish, swimming in the air. Molluscs, shell creatures, dolphins, whales and, across the room through all the stench and the noise and the seething movement, her. Sitting on a stool at the breakfast bar of his West Auckland three-bedroom Lockwood home talking to one of the snails he had stood on as a boy. He thought, 'Look up,' but she wouldn't look up.

He woke the next morning, still in the same chair, with a new-found optimism; he felt happy. He tried to pull himself down. He tried to tell himself what a bad man he was but the feeling wouldn't go away. It was there and it wouldn't go away. He was happy. There was a lightness about him that he couldn't explain. He thought he must be going to die, that this was some kind of emotional death throe, but it stayed, days, weeks, months. He knew he had no right to it but it infected him. He smiled and laughed and it weighed on him with a negative force that lifted him. It was like he was ageing backwards, like things were falling off him. It felt as though he would take off, float away – he checked himself in the mirrored windows of buildings. He still cared; it was like he had more room to care. During his lunch breaks he stood in gift shops choosing cards he thought his children would like. In the cards he wrote simple messages and put crisp twenty-dollar notes. He imagined the letters never reached them, but they would be older soon and then they could decide for themselves. He could sit with them and answer their questions. Hope lurked everywhere.

He had nowhere to go from here. Nowhere to go except sadness and loss. He knew the arc, he knew how it went, but he couldn't seem to be overly concerned by it, the pleasure was too deep. The existence too light and too happy, and too much joy surrounded him; he seemed completely involved with the joy like it was a job. It hit him, over and over again, everything seemed bright and full of promise. The longer it stayed the longer he suspected it would stay – with him, the murderer, the rapist, the two-timing deadbeat dad. Better people than him had nothing. Better people than him looked at their nothing and were grateful they didn't have too much to carry. Better people's children died, better people were killed and raped and two-timed and neglected and his lightness grew and grew and the more it grew the more

93

he wanted it, knowing the whole time that at any time it could leave but feeling like it would go on for ever and ever, and in the presence of better people crying and screaming out for even a moment's relief he just couldn't get sad. He knew he should but he just couldn't summon the want to want to. He rebelled at the thought of being sad, like a gag reflex, not consciously but deep down. He refused to let the lightness go. It was his, he said, like a child, a spoiled child. He walked, dizzy with it, to work, day after day, with hundreds of other people and he walked home until one day he stopped. The weight of him and everything above pressed his feet to the porous footpath and the ground, in return, pushed up to meet him. He looked from where he stood and noticed small things – hope, kindness – and smiled. He would write a letter tonight, to her. 'Far from leaving,' he would write, 'it's the fear of it leaving that has left.' I would skip, he thought, but it's not skipping I want, for his heart was grown-up now and rested in a new home.

Funny Too

Four of us are sitting in the sun, in a garden bar. There's Digby and me, Seamus and Rose and their twins. Digby, Seamus and I watch the kids running up and down the stairs. Rose is reading the Sunday paper.

Seamus tells a story. He says when he did music at school they played bells. Seamus's school spent a fortune on a set of hand-bells and the music class played "Goodnight Kiwi" on them at assemblies and old people's homes.

'Hine e Hine,' Rose says, without looking up from the paper.

Seamus says, 'Eh?'

'It's called "Hine e Hine".' She still doesn't look up; she licks her finger and turns the large newspaper page. 'The "Goodnight Kiwi" song.'

Seamus says none of them wanted to play the bells, the whole class just wanted to sit round with guitars and learn "Sweet Child O' Mine" by Guns N' Roses.

'I've seen photos,' Rose says. I can't work out how she's reading and listening at the same time but she looks like she is. 'He cheated in his grade two theory exam as well. He wrote on his pencil case in code.'

'It probably took longer to work out the code and remember what it stood for than it would have to study for the exams,' Seamus says.

'Is that what you're going to tell Mack and Sam?' Digby says, nodding toward the twins. They've just started school. We all laugh.

Rose says, 'How do you convince a jury in Christchurch that a police cadet raped a drug-addicted prostitute he'd already paid for sex?' It sounds like the set-up for a joke. It's not.

'Um, you don't?' Seamus says, looking at us and shrugging his shoulders.

Rose flicks the paper out straight again. 'He says being a police officer was his life-long dream. He started police college when he was thirty-one.' Mack comes over and takes a sip of water from a glass on the table. 'That's a long time to wait to fulfil a life-long dream.'

'Mack!' Seamus says, standing up. Mack is pouring the glass of water over Sam's shoes.

Rose looks up from the paper and says, 'Isn't it?' to us.

Digby and I walk home in the sun. On the way I'm laughing every now and then. Out loud, I go, 'Bing. BingBingBing. Bing, Bing, Bing – Bing,' ringing a pretend bell on one of the 'bings' and waiting in anticipation through the others. It wears thin and I have to run to catch up with

Digby who's waiting for the lights to change at the bypass so he can cross. I think about asking him what his life-long dream is, to make up for annoying him with the bell thing, but he says, 'Mack and Sam are funny, eh?' The lights take ages so I say, 'But I'm funny too, eh?'

Mary's Job

It was the Saturday night before Christmas. Mary sat at her desk looking at her computer screen. The light above her cubicle was the only one on. The rest of the floor was in darkness.

She'd started a publish at two that afternoon. It took five hours to get new content onto the test site. She'd gone to a costume party at seven. She thought she'd just be popping into work to check the test site and push it to live, but now she sat looking at the report on her screen. The publishing system had deleted a thousand pages off the test site and the number was flicking over higher and higher as she watched: 1,207, 1,245, 1,269. There were about 9,000 pages on the ministry's website. It would stop soon, she thought – she'd been thinking since the report read 800. Mary looked out the window then back at the screen – 1,503 – it would stop soon. She'd call technical support when it got to 1,700, maybe

2,000. She looked at the time, ten fifteen. She didn't want to call tech support at ten fifteen on a Saturday night. The ministry outsourced maintenance of the publishing system. She put on her headset and rang tech support. The way things were going it'd be 1,700 by the time she finished dialling.

'How many?'

'Simon, hi, sorry to . . .'

'How many?' Simon said.

'1,712 . . . 13 . . . 14 . . .'

'Hilarious.'

Mary heard Simon shift from his chair and walk to another room.

'What's gone?' he asked.

Mary scrolled through the report. 'All the legislation, most of the forms and all the letters off the internal site.' She watched as Simon stopped the publish and the report slowed, then stood still. '1,812,' she said.

'We have a winner,' Simon said.

'It's getting worse.'

'Ya think?' Simon said, then, 'Damn,' under his breath.

She heard typing and mouse-shifting and began to swing in her chair.

'Did you go as Gabriel in the end?' Simon said.

'Yeah.' Mary picked at the silk Greek-style dress she was wearing.

'Feathers or cellophane?'

'Feather ones.' Mary looked at the wings on the chair beside her.

'Very Victoria's Secret.'

'Yeah, without them I kind of just look like Jane Austen. There were three of us.' There was silence over the phone except for the typing. 'Gabriels.'

'Did you have an archangel cage fight?'

'Don't get weird,' Mary said.

'You better get a cup of tea,' Simon said.

'Is it going to take a while?'

Mary padded to the kitchenette in bare feet, her long dress sweeping the floor and floating out behind her. It was warm in the building; the air conditioning was turned off on Friday at about midnight and back on at four o'clock on Monday morning. It made the whole place a new type of quiet. When she worked late she could tell time by the level of silence. It was wetter without the air conditioning. As the jug boiled she took hair clips out of her hair. She shook her head and glitter rained on the bench. Her hair stayed in place. The sign above the sink said, 'Your mother doesn't work here – wash your own dishes!' She heard her phone ring.

'How committed are you to this publish?' Simon said.

'Oh, that sounds like what I want to hear.'

'I'm just asking.'

'The changes have to be on the website by 8.00 a.m. Monday.'

'Or what?' Simon said.

'There could be some discomfort.'

'Yeah, but, no one's going to die,' Simon said. 'It's not brain surgery.'

There was silence for a moment.

'The CEO wants the changes on the site by Monday

at 8.00 a.m.,' Mary said. There was more silence and the sound of Simon waiting. 'The CEO came down on Friday and said he wanted them on the site by 8.00 a.m. Monday.'

'Do you like your job?' Simon said.

'Not at eleven o'clock on a Saturday night, dressed as an angel.'

'Archangel.'

'Sorry, archangel.'

'I think I might be able to find a way of limping on.'

Mary looked at the ceiling, rows and rows of holes in tiles. 'With all due respect Simon, isn't "limping on" what got us here in the first place?'

'Don't go all "due respect" on me. Do you want a publish or not?'

'I want a publish without some huckery fix holding that publish together.'

'You can't have both,' Simon said.

Mary looked out the window. A sled with reindeer flashed on and off.

'Then I guess I want a publish,' she said. 'I'm not manually republishing eighteen hundred pages, though.'

'Eighteen hundred and twelve,' Simon said.

'I'm not manually republishing eighteen hundred and twelve pages.'

'Nah. Just don't push it to live.'

'Ya think?' Mary said.

'Yeah,' he said sarcastically, 'because with all due respect, Mary, if you do that we'll lose at least eighteen hundred and twelve pages off the live site.'

Mary rubbed her face and more glitter came off in

her hands. Simon started typing on the other end of the phone.

'Mary,' he said. 'Why didn't you go as Mary?'

'Should I leave you to this?'

'Nah, I need you to watch the report – I'm at home, I haven't got access to the report.'

'Home?' Mary said. 'I'm on the seventh floor of a corporate building on a Saturday night.'

'Don't jump off.'

'You didn't say Simon says.'

'It's implicit.'

Mary looked out the window. The city spread out, then stopped abruptly at the water. 'I'm going for a bit,' she said. 'I left my tea in the kitchen.'

'Tea,' Simon said. 'All right for some.'

'Get yourself a cup of tea, Simon.'

'Don't go far. I'll ring you.'

Mary pushed the end button on her phone and turned in her chair with her headset still on. The floor was running a 'decorate your cubicle' competition for Christmas. Her team hadn't started yet. They were all dealing with the cannibalising publishing system. Mary was a translator; the rest of her team produced content for the website. They went to people in the ministry, asked them what they needed, then wrote pages to go on the website. When there was a problem they came to her and she went to the technical people and explained their problem in technical terms. Then she went back to her team and explained the solution in non-technical terms. She looked at the box of business cards on her desk. They literally called her a Translator. People used to make things. She'd been brought in after a couple of altercations that escalated to written warnings, at least one of them addressed to Simon. Her boss, Robyn, said technical people weren't people-people, they were logic-people; communication was never a technical person's strength. Mary's main task was to talk to Simon, so no one else had to. He was the most difficult person in the technical team to deal with, because he was the one they relied on the most. For years he'd been cobbling together fixes to keep the publishing system functioning. By the time anyone realised this, he was the only one who actually knew how it was working. Simon displayed the arrogance of a failure. Mary imagined his mother saying things to him like 'They're only jealous.' People disliked him.

It had all gone underground since the publishing system had started deleting content. People stopped hushed conversations when Mary approached them. It started slowly, so no one had noticed. Then complaints started piling in: broken links, call-centre staff unable to find content, then the minister's office. A few people, including Mary, knew exactly what was wrong; no one knew how to fix it. Everyone blamed Simon. There were rumours and conjecture and finger-pointing. It wasn't the first time Mary had been in the office late and alone – it wasn't even the tenth. The publishing system had always been an ugly, dysfunctioning child that needed constant reassurance and direction. This was how she explained it to the rest of her team: 'You know Frankenstein's monster?' They joked about getting her an apartment in the block next door and making a trap-door for her to crawl through in the night. Her team called the publishing system 'her baby'. Simon called it a badly deformed abomination he'd inherited from another company that knew nothing. He talked constantly about what he would have done differently. Mary listened, ate almonds and said, 'Aha. Yip. Aha,' and when he was finished asked if he could do something for her. When he said yes, she'd make a joke with him and they'd laugh. People who didn't understand her job thought Mary was Simon's friend.

Her phone rang.

'Simon,' she said.

'How did you know it was me?'

'Everyone else I know is at a party,' Mary said.

'There's something wrong. I can only find one page altered.'

'Yeah,' Mary said, 'that's okay.'

'Eh?'

'We're only altering one page.'

'We're deleting eighteen hundred documents . . .'

'Eighteen hundred and twelve.'

'We're breaking the publishing freeze to alter one page?' Mary could hear him scrolling. 'The home page?' Simon said. 'We're breaking the publishing freeze to change the home page?'

'How's the fix going?'

'It's a Christmas message.'

'I've run out of almonds. I'm ready to go home.'

'It's a Christmas message from the CEO.'

She could hear Simon leaning back in his chair.

'Out of almonds, Simon.'

'Merry Fucking Christmas,' Simon said.

'I'm not talking to you about this, Simon. I'm talking

to you about the fix and that's what I'm talking to you about – and almonds.' She started looking through the drawers of her desk for more almonds.

'It must be great working for the public service, Mary – standing up, making a difference,' Simon said. 'Now, as an employee of an evil multinational corporation I don't care what it is I'm doing at eleven o'clock on a Saturday night, it's all money to a bread-head like me, but you, Mary, look at you, you're really making a difference.'

'I am literally squeezing a stress-ball, Simon,' said Mary. 'You have reduced me to cliché. What's happening with the fix?'

Simon hung up.

No one in Mary's family understood what Mary did for a job. They understood the translating thing, but they weren't sure what it was all for. What did she do? She tried to explain it was like management and her father said, 'Oh, so you're a manager?' and her parents' faces brightened a little. She said no, she wasn't anything like a manager – it wasn't like management.

She would get excited sometimes and ring her father and say, 'Check out the site, there's new stuff on the website.' He liked music and pictures. A few months ago one of the Communications team had brought up an armful of T-shirts. They were cleaning out the cupboard, did anyone want a T-shirt? The T-shirts said things like 'Get moving' and 'Move it or lose it'. They'd been printed for the ministry's team in the Corporate Challenge. Three hundred public servants walking and running through the streets of Wellington to show a commitment to work/life balance. Mary had sent one of the T-shirts to her father. Every time she'd talked to him since, he said it was the best T-shirt he had. He was wearing it to the gym; could she send him another one? It was such great cotton.

The phone rang within the half hour.

'I just thought of something,' Simon said. 'I wonder if you can help me out with this, I think I have it straight. So we're not breaking the publishing freeze for the Select Committee information to let people make informed submissions, but we are breaking it for a Christmas message?'

'Wearing thin, Simon,' she said.

'This must irk you, Ms Mary.'

'It has Santa on it,' said Mary. 'How could anything with Santa irk me.'

'Your Te Reo resources can't go up – but a Christmas message can?'

'PC gone sane, Simon. What can I say?'

'Your job sucks,' he laughed and hung up.

It was his fault. She tried to be nice and say, 'Oh, no maybe it was us. We push the publishing system so hard. We were bound to break something eventually,' but it was his fault. All his dodgy fixes had made the publishing system eat itself and when he said, 'Yeah, it was probably you,' she was pretty sure he knew it was his fault.

Ten minutes later, he sent Mary an email saying, 'Tin a cocoa. Tin a cocoa. PC never looked good on you.' This was how he tried to secure her allegiance. It was like he watched other people being friendly, tried to replicate it and got it all wrong. 'We're like the Odd Couple,' he once said to Mary. 'You're a liberal and I'm a realist.' She drank cold tea from her white mug and thought, this is my job.

On Friday, Robyn had asked Mary to join her in the General Manager's office. They'd explained the CEO's request and asked if she could organise it. A month before, they'd promised technical support a publishing freeze until the New Year. No new content going on, no old content coming off, so they could concentrate on fixing the problem. Mary took notes in a hard-covered exercise book and said, 'Yeah, sure.' Robyn had faith in her completely; this meeting was for the benefit of the General Manager. The website was making him look bad. Mary closed her book and, looking out the window, said, 'There are risks.' The General Manager had said, 'I don't want to hear about risks, I just want it done.' Mary stood for the website and all the things about the website he didn't understand. All the things he didn't understand were the things making him look bad.

The phone rang.

'Happy Holidays.' She imagined Simon, sitting in his office at home, doing whatever he did, suddenly thinking of it and saying to himself, 'I must share that with Mary. We like to have each other on. That's what friends do.'

'Simon.' For all she knew the fix was finished and he was pissing about.

'Isn't that what you liberals say?' Simon said. 'It says "Merry Christmas", you know, Mary? Isn't that a bit denominational? There's a picture of Santa on it.'

'And a small robin holding a sprig of holly.'

'Do you want to call the PC Police or shall I?'

Suddenly she didn't feel like being nice any more.

'Simon, you don't seem to be getting much done towards this fix – shall I call Robyn?'

There was a pause.

'Robyn's in Hawera,' Simon said.

'It's okay, I've got her cell phone number,'

'Give me half an hour or so.' Simon hung up.

Mary took off her head set and said 'Fuck you' to the phone. She flicked the space bar of her keyboard with her index finger. She could push the test site to live and destroy the whole website – she could say it was an accident, it was late, Simon was annoying – she'd warned them. She could have asked a question in the General Manager's office. She could have said, 'The risk outweighs the benefit.' She could have said, 'I feel uncomfortable with this.' She could have said, 'This is crazy.'

The cubicle across the floor, Actuaries, was decorated with sand, towels and a tent. The banner above it said 'New Zealand Christmas'. Human Resources had fastened white fluffy snow to everything. They had a snowman in the centre of their cubicle. The lawyers had cut out paper to make some sort of Santa's grotto. People used to build things for a living; her father built houses. She lay down on the couch outside the General Manager's office and read a women's magazine she found on his PA's desk. Her phone rang at 1:45 a.m. She let it ring, then walked slowly towards her desk, still in bare feet, dress floating behind her.

'I thought you'd gone home,' Simon said.

'Lindsay Lohan's in rehab,' she said.

'Robert Downey's out.'

'Wow, is it, like, 1995 at your house?' Mary flicked through the magazine. She was the boss now.

'It's done,' said Simon. 'You can run the publish again. Have you still got it all in the profile?'

Mary moved her mouse and looked at the screen as she stood behind her desk, 'Um, yup.'

'Okay, start the publish. Merry Fucking . . .'

'Simon, you've done that one already.'

'You can go home,' he said. 'Come back in the morning and push it to live.'

'Yeah,' Mary stretched. 'I'll call you if there are any problems.'

'There won't be any problems.'

'Have a good sleep Simon,' she said. 'Talk to you tomorrow.'

'Hopefully not.'

'True story.' She picked up her wings from the chair beside her.

'See ya,' Simon said.

'Thanks.'

The next morning when she came in the test site was intact. She emailed Simon to say 'All well,' and pushed the test site to live. On Monday afternoon, identical boxes wrapped in identical ribbon were delivered to every staff member on Mary's floor. There was a card in each box saying, 'Thanks for your good work,' with the ministry's stamp below. One of Mary's team said, 'Oh look, it's like the whole ministry's wishing us Merry Christmas.' The box contained a beach towel, some sunblock, a torch with an alarm and an AM/FM radio.

'What's the handle for?' Mary said, playing with the small black handle on the side of the torch.

'You can wind it up to charge it,' Robyn said. 'It's for your survival kit at home.'

Mary wound the handle and it made a whirring noise. Her father would like the beach towel and she might send the sunblock to Simon – for Christmas.

You Might Be Right

'We're vegan.' He says it, kind of waving his hand to indicate he means all of us: me, him and the baby. 'We don't have any animal products.' They smile. We sent an email earlier. Before we got here – to Samoa – we sent an email to the hotel to check we could eat something. The person we sent it to sent it to the maître-d', who sent it to the chef, who sent it back to the person we sent it to, who sent it back to us, saying, 'This should be fine. Not a problem.' The manager, the person we sent it to originally, forgot to delete the messages underneath his. He had forwarded our email to the maître-d' with a message saying, 'Get a load of this *grin*.' The maître-d' forwarded our email and the manager's message to the chef saying, 'Sorry – this is bound to be a pain in the arse.'

We feel bad before we get there. We take silver packs of soy protein and vegetarian luncheon sausage. I feel like a spaceman. Everyone we know who was vegan is freegan now. People say we care more about animals than people. I watch a documentary showing someone killing baby cats – kittens. One of the last vegans I know says she can't watch it. She says vegans should be exempt from watching it. Someone else says that's shit, if she expects other people to watch it she should watch it herself. I hate cats. I watch about ten seconds more of the documentary and I can't watch it any more. They poison some dogs with cyanide. The dogs look like frightened children. I don't particularly like children either. When I meet people I try to wait as long as possible before I tell them – about the vegan thing. Most people don't like children particularly – or cats.

We go for a drive. We rent a car, pack up our vegetarian luncheon sausage and some white, bouncy bread and we go for a drive. There are dogs everywhere. I send an email home, saying, 'We're having a great time; there are dogs everywhere in Samoa.' A lot of the dogs have bits missing: ears, eyes, legs. On Savai'i, while we're waiting for the ferry, a group of them surround us like a 1980s horror movie. The baby teases them from her car seat. She shows them her vegetarian luncheon sausage and they growl. We say, 'Don't worry the dogs.' They look like they have rabies. Neither of us have seen a dog with rabies, but we agree these dogs look like they have rabies. We wind up the windows and drive somewhere else to wait for the ferry.

For dinner we eat palusami and taro chips. We stay in a fale on Savai'i and eat curry and rice. We eat more palusami. Palusami quickly becomes our favourite food. I have my photo taken outside the Marlon Brando fale.

We meet Aggie Grey's granddaughter – she dances for us. There is fire every night: fire-dancing, fire-twirling, and jumping from the top of a palm tree into the swimming pool holding fire. We eat more palusami and lots of star fruit. We see pawpaw growing on trees. Anywhere else I've been I hate pawpaw, but I can eat it in Samoa with pleasure. Everywhere we go it rains – big, fat, warm rain. I had a different holiday in mind. I thought it would be sunny all the time and I would be lounging by the pool, getting brown, but it rains and often isn't swimming weather. We try to go snorkelling. We take the baby out a wee way, and I see a fish and panic and don't go snorkelling any more. I think of *Jaws* and *Piranha* and *Piranha 2*, where they could fly. I don't like fish. I don't like animals where I can't see them – where they can creep up on me. On the way to the snorkelling beach we see a dead dog – stiff, with its legs up. We agree someone will come for it. On the way home it's still there, only fatter. It'll burst if the sun stays out. It's in a ditch.

They have a huge banquet that night, Aggie Grey's granddaughter dances again. There's fish everywhere, raw fish marinated in coconut milk and fresh limes. I think about the fish that were there while we were snorkelling – how sneaking up on someone and frightening them isn't a nice thing to do. There are shellfish. Shellfish are like vegetables to me. 'No central nervous system,' I say to the baby. I order palusami and a vegetarian pizza with no cheese and can they check there is no butter or milk in the pizza base. The waiter smiles. I feel elite in the worst way. We all eat palusami and taro chips, the baby gets some of it in her hair and tries to feed the rest of it to a cat that lives in the hotel. The pizza has parmesan on it, so I order some more palusami. The parmesan is a test, an accident or a misunderstanding. I leave the pizza untouched hoping that someone will eat it in the kitchen. Waste, food miles, hypocrisy, reliance on capitalism, elitism – someone mentions one of these things to me most days. In New Zealand the doctor says 'restricted diet' a couple of times and I figure sooner or later someone is going to take the baby off us. The Plunket Nurse says, 'Just a glass of milk a day would do it.' I think about a million cows in pain and all the rivers drowned in shit and say, 'Yeah, that would do it.' I start lying to the Plunket Nurse. I say, 'Yeah,' when she says, 'Is she having any meat?' The baby has never seen meat. I stop going to see the Plunket Nurse. Someone asks me if I've ever given the baby a choice to eat meat. While we're in Samoa the baby eats pigeon shit and some weird fluffy plant. I say, 'Yeah, nah, I haven't done that.' I say I see their point, but I don't, not really. I pretend to cooperate. I say, 'You might be right.' It's my secret way of not getting into a fight when I don't agree with someone. The nutritionist at the hospital tells me I have to go back to Plunket. I say, 'Okay,' but I might as well have said, 'You might be right.' The baby and I walk back through the hospital carpark, there's a cold and dry wind. 'It's warm enough in Samoa to grow beans and wet enough to grow rice,' I tell her. 'That's a perfect protein – pulses and grain.' If I could catch a wild pig with my bare hands and kill it with my bare hands and eat it raw I probably would.

One overcast day in Samoa we go to Robert Louis Stevenson's estate. There are fireplaces in most of the rooms. We walk up the hill in Roman sandals to the memorial. Black lizards move as we walk close to them. At first I think I'm seeing things, from the lack of protein and iron, and the humidity, and the long walk uphill, but then we see them and they join us and the baby laughs and tries to catch the lizards with her bare, hungry hands.

The Other Side of the World

Her mother was coming from the other side of the world. As she sat in her bed in the bedroom of her London flat, Beth imagined her mother – coming from the other side of the world. Driving to the airport with her father, parking the car, checking in. She would have bought something to put her tickets in, something that hung around her neck or tied up around her waist. Someone would have said they were good. Beth's father would have made her check over and over again that she had her tickets and her passport and her credit card. She would take the thing out from under her clothing and check it and then return it and then she would go through the gates. Beth's sister, Clare, would meet her at Heathrow. Clare would fly from Melbourne and their mother would fly from Auckland and they would meet at Heathrow and take a taxi or the underground. It was easy on the train but they would probably take a taxi. Both of them would be tired by the time they got to Beth's flat. She had nothing to eat and if she did it would be no use. Her sister would need to go shopping, perhaps her mother would cook. Beth couldn't face it. Hopefully, no one would say she needed to keep her strength up. Micah and the children had left three weeks ago. It was as fast as they could pull it all together. Her mother was travelling almost completely on Clare and Rowena's air-points. Rowena had organised time off work to look after their father. It was a massive undertaking. Everyone was enjoying the organising. Beth hadn't been involved. There had been a telephone call and it had taken off from there, like snow falling. No one had asked her. Clare had said, 'Don't be silly,' and that was that.

Beth hadn't tidied. Since Micah had left she hadn't tidied. The flat was dirty. She thought about getting up to clean it and then she thought again. He wasn't going to sit around and watch her die and he didn't think it was good for the children to do so either.

'You've brought this on yourself,' he said. If only she'd be more positive about things. It was anger that was eating her up, anger and fear, and if she was doing nothing to resolve it he couldn't let it infect the rest of them. It seems cruel, he'd written, but it's for the best, for all of us. She had fought and he had remained reasonable and then she hit Tess and he saw it and Tess made it worse than it was, like ten-year-olds will, and when Beth came home the next day there was a note and some money and the flat was empty. It was like a bad book. It didn't even feel like a dream, it was so mundane. It felt like daytime TV. No one should have to put up with that from anyone, he wrote. Violence is never an answer for anyone, no matter what they've brought on themselves. She had the note. It had a phone number on it. He called sometimes to let the children talk to her but she never picked up. She was tired, and now her mother and sister were coming.

She didn't want them there. She didn't really care, though. She was tired and bored and it all just floated in and out now, day after day. Like a parade of one brass band after another. They could come. They were in the air now. There would be noise and she would nod and there would be fights and she would sigh and clench her teeth and then there would be eating and perhaps they would want to take her out. It wasn't much to ask, Beth thought, three months at the most, it didn't seem like much to ask out of someone's life. But he was gone now. He'd taken Tess and Stevie and he'd gone and who could blame him? Violence is never an answer and the children needed their father.

'You're not still reading these horrible books?' Clare was visiting from Melbourne. She was going to a conference delivering a paper on causation; no one really understood what Clare did. Beth was pregnant with Stevie, Tess was in childcare. Clare and Beth had spent the afternoon eating, Clare drinking wine.

'I think I've eaten myself into a stupor,' Beth had said and they both laughed. They couldn't stop laughing. Beth went to the toilet and when she came back Clare was at the bookshelf reading the back of a book and asked again, 'You're not still into all this, are you?' And they both laughed again.

They'd gone to the Serpentine. Micah could pick up Tess. Clare walked slowly so Beth could keep up. She felt huge, like Queen Victoria. The gallery was showing paintings by John Currin.

'It makes me like people again,' Beth said, then corrected herself. 'Paintings of people. I always think I like landscapes' – they were looking at a painting of two women laughing – 'but I really do like paintings of people.'

It had started when Beth left school. She went to work for a couple who went to a Spiritualist Church and told her things like 'There's more' and 'You can have anything you want'. It was true. Beth had asked and it had been provided, including Micah. She'd written down everything she wanted on a piece of paper that she burned in a bonfire in her backyard. 'If nothing else, you'll know it when you see it,' someone had said, and they were right. Micah had been cynical and then he started to see it working so he asked and it was all provided, including the understanding of it. They glowed as a couple. They shone and they smiled. Clare had asked, the night of the Serpentine Gallery, while they sat around Micah and Beth's table eating salad and rice. 'It's like,' Micah said, 'the other day I was in a taxi going to the airport and we got one green light after another and the taxi driver commented on it and I thought, this is like my life.'

'All green lights,' Beth said and held his hand.

It didn't seem right to Clare. 'What about the people waiting at the red lights?' she asked.

'Everyone needs to look after themselves,' Beth said. 'You can't look after anyone else, not really. It just doesn't work like that. We all choose.'

119

They'd bought a postcard at the gallery of the two women laughing and it had been tucked into a book for ages and then it wasn't.

Clare had said it was a bad match from the beginning. She said 'I told you so' to their mother more than once after Micah left. Her mother said that wasn't the issue now. She should come home, how could they get Beth home? 'You talk to her,' their mother said, and Clare did. There was no way she was coming home. There was no way she was going anywhere, she said, and they laughed, Beth for real and Clare to be polite. 'Are you sure it wouldn't be better?' Clare asked. Beth was sure it wouldn't be better. She needed to be there, close to things. She couldn't face the flight. 'Everyone should just stay where they are,' Beth said. Clare said, 'Don't be silly,' and it was decided. Her mother asked if Beth had tried to get hold of Micah, and Beth said no, in a tired way that made her mother defensive. 'Surely you want to see the kids?' she said. 'Why?' asked Beth and her mother said, 'Well,' and then neither of them said anything for a moment.

Clare tried to contact Micah. Her mother advised against it but she tried. She waited up late one Thursday night until she thought it might be about eleven o'clock in the morning in London. She called his work and he wouldn't take her call. She called his cell phone and he said, 'Clare, I really don't think we have anything to discuss here.' It seemed cruel to Clare, worse than cruel. He said it would. Beth has become violent, he wrote in an email that Clare suspected was designed to explain things, but which made no sense. He didn't expect it to,

Micah wrote, but he'd spoken with a lawyer and he was well within his rights. The children were fine and if she wanted, while she and her mother were in town they could see them, but not with Beth, and then something about energy and the weight of psychic contamination. He was sorry, but he couldn't help Beth if she wouldn't help herself.

Beth had a sore back. She would move around while they were eating dinner, trying to get comfortable. She'd switch from haunch to haunch but it wouldn't go away. She meditated at first, meditated on everything being right in her world. She said affirmations to try and shift the energy that was blocked in her body. When people noticed her wincing she said, 'I'm letting go of something.' After a while she took paracetamol, then ibuprofen, then codeine. Then she went to the doctor. On the way to the doctor she tried to find change for the bus, she was sure there was some in the bottom of her handbag. She pulled out four packets of different painkillers and, wedged in the corner of her handbag, a quartz crystal and a small piece of paper saying, 'All is well with me and my world.'

There wasn't anything they could do. 'Medically,' Micah had said when the doctor told them, 'you can't do anything, medically.' Micah made an appointment at an aura specialist. It was anger, the woman said, anger and fear. She asked Beth to lie down: she needed to be still. Beth's back hurt as the woman shook things and waved things over her. Everything that had made sense didn't. Micah stuck the affirmations all over the house and they weren't allowed to mention it to anyone. 'The word *sick*

will not be used in this house,' he said. 'It's very important.'
The only thought she had was, I am going to die. When
he held her and said, 'We're beating this' she thought: I
won't see my children's next birthdays. All felt lost. She
tried to claw it back but there was something new living
in her head and she begged him to let her tell the children.
'What good will come of that?' he said, and he was right.
She wanted it to not be happening and Micah said he was
doing everything he could to stop it happening and she
needed to do that too. One afternoon Micah came home
and she was in bed with someone else and drunk. She
said, 'So what?' like it was his fault. Micah went back to
the aura specialist alone. The woman said what he didn't
understand, what he had no conception of, was that his
fear, his negativity, had the power to actually kill Beth.
That night he sat at the dining table they had eaten over
and passed plates over, the table they had weaned both
their children at and repeated to himself over and over
that all was well.

In the morning, after everyone left, Beth started
drinking again. She pulled down all the pieces of paper
from the walls, leaving small clumps of Blu-Tack with
paper corners stuck to them. When he came home she'd
hit him, told him to fuck off and then she hit Tess. She
knocked the ten-year-old over with a blow to the side
of her head and they left. It was better for everyone this
way. She was the child now. Her father couldn't afford to
come so she would say goodbye to him over the phone,
and Rowena, both of them, in the small house he and
their mother had moved into after all the girls had left.
He'd bought a new television and that would keep him

company while his wife was away, and he'd have the garden and he'd call soon and he loved her. She was tired. If she might ask something for the others, if it might work like that in this one thing – make her well.

Christchurch

We drive into town and I say 'I hate this city' – over and over and with increasing venom. Everything I see, I remember another reason to hate it. When we get to the car park we see some people I don't like the look of and that's it; their tiny heads, their red necks. I say, 'It's so cold here, no one leaves their family home to breed.' You sigh and I get the message and finish by saying, 'I lived here for five years and that was four and a half years too long.' We find a park on the third floor. There are 150 parks left in the building and it costs $1.10 for every hour of parking and you say, 'Does that change your mind?' and I say, 'Nah.' We get the pushchair out of the boot. I have cold feet. It's been years since I've had cold feet. You say your legs are cold. I put the baby's jacket on over the top of the pushchair straps. She can't move so I have to take it off and put it on all over again. As we walk to the lift I look at the hills stretched out to breaking and I say, 'Hard to beat those hills though.' You look out over them and say,

'Yeah – the sky goes on forever.' You've hit the nail on the head – the birds don't disappear here. You can watch them all the way to the Alps. Washing takes all day to dry if it doesn't freeze solid on the line. People stay here and the river runs beside them staying.

We see women getting out of European cars wearing fur and Italian boots. It's like someone's set it up just for me to hate and I say, 'Told you so.' You laugh at me. I say, 'What?' You say, 'Just you.' It feels like that here. I try to point it out – the rich and white. 'Where are the brown people?' I say, and you point to someone and I say, 'What about the Chinese people? Huh? Huh?' You laugh again and it's still just me. The baby's kicking off her boots – over and over. I end up putting them on the handles of the push-chair. Nothing's changed. People are dead and they've been replaced by more and more people just like them. It's like a video game based on a zombie film.

We have lunch at a café and they serve us a huge pile of mashed potatoes and mushrooms. You look at it, and say, 'It's not a meal you'd cook yourself.' They put whipped cream in cups of filtered coffee and call it a Vienna. The baby eats last night's dinner. She sneaks up on a businessman in a suit and tries to steal his ID card which is on a retractable cord. It retracts. I say sorry, and he says, 'Do you want to work at Telecom?' He's talking to the baby. I say, 'I'm sure she'd work hard,' and he looks at me like I'm trying to find a job for my child. I remind him he brought it up. He smiles. The baby walks away and finds an expensive fur coat on the back of a chair. She thinks it's alive, which it was once. 'Like everything else in this city,' I say to her but she pretends not to understand.

A Noisy Place

There were seven inmates at the AA meeting and three women from AA on the outside. The women from outside wore coats with keys in their pockets. They folded and unfolded their visitor's slips around their driver's licences. It wasn't church. Church was on Wednesdays but one woman spoke at a time and none of the inmates spoke for long. The first AA woman talked about being in her own personal prison when she was drinking and how AA set her free. After she finished, Poppy asked to be excused to go to the toilet. The AA women smiled and nodded. There was one guard covering the whole wing and the AA people asked that they didn't come into the room for head-counts because it was anonymous. The prison social worker agreed and the guards were instructed just to check from the window in the door occasionally – to make sure no one was hurting anyone else.

Poppy shut the half-door of the toilet stall and sat against it. She closed her eyes and listened to the hum of noise far enough away to be nothing. Prison was a noisy place. There was always talk – the shit women talk – over and over, for years and years: they didn't do it, their kids, their kids being molested, their kids in CYFS care, their kids being molested in CYFS care, Jesus, dreams, standovers, TV, boyfriends, girlfriends, who's holding, losing things, swapping things, parole, excuses, no parole.

'Poppy?' It was Slade, looking over the stall. 'Poppy – all I'm saying is if she's been transferred, why did she get sick so fast?'

'And all I'm saying is stop saying it to me,' said Poppy, standing up.

'It makes sense.'

'Slade – with respect and without any desire to get involved – it sounds paranoid.'

'She's a narc.'

'She's hanging out.' Her voice began to whine.

'She's a cop,' Slade said.

'Then tell someone.'

'I'm telling you.'

'What do you want me to do about it?'

Slade didn't know.

'What do you think you should do about it?' Slade said.

'Nothing. I'm going back to AA.'

They were reading the book when Poppy and Slade got back. The meeting took an hour. At the end they all held hands, said a prayer and the AA women hugged everyone and left. The guard came to take Poppy and Slade back to their cell and lock them down for the night.

As they walked through the door of their cell Slade said, 'You're wrong,' in a way that only Poppy could hear. Grace was lying on the camp stretcher.

The cell could fit one inmate comfortably, two at a pinch. Poppy had been in prison for ten years, five of them in this cell with Slade. Then, two weeks ago, the maintenance people brought a camp stretcher and Grace had arrived, carrying her plastic bag. She said she'd been transferred from a prison up north. She started sniffing and coughing and shaking about three days in. Slade watched a lot of TV. She didn't believe Grace had been transferred from another prison. Slade was convinced Grace had the flu and if she'd been transferred from another prison she wouldn't get the flu. 'Institutional immunity,' she said. It was straw-clutching to say the least. She'd been explaining it to Poppy for a week and each time she explained it Slade became more convinced of it. It was crazy. Neither Poppy nor Slade was anyone. Poppy had been someone but wasn't now. Slade was someone on the outside but not here. Slade was mad and Poppy was tired.

Grace coughed.

'You need to cover your mouth when you cough,' Slade said. No one said anything else and the lights went out. In the dark, women shouted goodnights to each other across the wing. Someone sang. Someone cried. Toilets flushed. Grace covered her mouth and coughed.

The next day two jobs came up in the sewing room. Poppy was given a second chance and Slade was offered the other job. When the supervisor briefed them, she said Poppy would have to start on the screenprinting because she needed to build trust again after last time, with the machines and the scissors.

They made grey marl sweatshirts and pants for the men's prisons. Poppy screened *CORRECTIONS DEPT* in black over and over again on the backs of the sweatshirts.

Lunch was one creamed corn sandwich and one luncheon sausage sandwich wrapped so tight in Glad Wrap the white bread was almost dough again. On the way back to the cells, Poppy swapped her luncheon for a corn with a woman who owed her money. That woman swapped it back for a corn with a woman who knew her mum. Slade caught her up.

'Didn't think you'd ever get back in the sewing room, eh?' said Slade.

Poppy looked at her sandwiches.

'Lucky,' said Slade.

'You want corn?' said Poppy.

'Us both – imagine that? Out of everyone here, we get a sewing job,' Slade said.

'Corn's my favourite but you can have it,' Poppy said.

'Leaving Grace alone in the cell sniffing around.'

Poppy held out the sandwich and looked at Slade for the first time.

'Oh – go on then.' Slade took the sandwich. 'You want luncheon?' Poppy shook her head.

Back in the cell they watched *Dr Phil* and Grace looked sicker than yesterday. Slade didn't say anything.

'You been to the nurse, Grace?' Poppy said.

'Nah, I'm just hanging out.' Grace looked at the TV.

Poppy looked at Slade to say, see, she's not sick, she just needs drugs.

'Yeah,' Grace added, 'one of you couldn't put me right on that, could you?'

Slade looked at Poppy to say, see, she's a narc pretending she needs drugs but she's sick. Slade said to Grace, 'We wouldn't know anything about any of that.'

Grace shrugged. 'Oh well, maybe I'll come to AA with you fellas next week.'

'Don't ask again,' Slade said.

The door opened, it was the twelve thirty muster.

'Brown?' the guard shouted.

'Miss.'

'Durham?'

'Miss.'

'Fields?'

'Miss.'

'Fields, you need to get those clothes off the floor.'

'Yes, Miss,' said Grace.

She hauled herself off the stretcher, picked up her clothes and put them in her drawer, saying 'Fucking screws.'

Poppy laughed. 'It's not *Bad Girls*, Grace.'

'It's all right for you. It sucks here.'

'It's prison,' Poppy said.

'It's boring.' Grace coughed and coughed and spat and shut up.

'I'm onto you,' Slade said.

'What?' said Grace.

'Nothing,' said Poppy.

After lunch, a guard took Slade and Poppy back to the sewing room. Poppy wondered, by two o'clock, how many shirts would equal enough trust to get her back on a machine or cutting or anything that wasn't screenprinting.

She tried to listen closely to the noise of the sewing machines as they fell into a rhythm of distance; a sleeve, a neckline, a waist-band. She tried to follow enough of them for a continual hum. Then she tried to pick out just the high part so it stung her head. A woman bumped into her as she went past and said 'Watch out, Poppy Tea,' like she was looking for a fight. If she was, it was with the wrong person.

At four o'clock, everyone from the wing was let out in the yard for an hour. Poppy smoked and read a book in a corner away from everyone. Grace slapped hands and talked shit. Slade ran round and round the tiny yard surrounded by fencing and razor wire. When Poppy looked up from her book to see where the sun had gone she saw Slade talking to a woman. The woman was someone; Slade was shaking her head while she talked to her.

One of the guards organised a volleyball game in the gym. The gym echoed and banged. The guard's keys rattled as she played and a couple of times her two-way radio fell out of its holster. Slade came over and raised her eyebrow to the woman standing next to Poppy on the court. The woman left and Slade took her place. When they rotated to the baseline, Poppy said, 'What was that about?'

'Taking care of business,' said Slade.

The ball came to Poppy and she batted at it awkwardly. The woman in front of her dove and got it over the net.

'Someone knew what to do,' said Slade. The ball flew behind Poppy and bounced in. The diving woman yelled, 'Fuck!' and, 'If you're playing, Poppy, play. If you're not, let Grace play.' Grace heard her name and ran over, coughing. Poppy got the cigarette from behind her ear and walked to the door.

'Please, Miss,' she said, lifting the cigarette to indicate to the guard by the door. The guard let her back into the yard, shouting 'Durham!' behind her.

At dinner that night, Poppy and Slade sat at the same table in silence. They ate off their trays looking at their food all the time.

'Something on your mind Poppy?'

'Nah.' Poppy shook her head.

Slade buttered a piece of white bread with a plastic knife.

'Just,' Poppy wiped her mouth with a serviette, 'just, things have been quiet for us for a while now, eh?'

Slade nodded.

'No trouble?' said Poppy.

'What's your point?'

'Well, things are good like that – aren't they?'

'Are they?' said Slade.

Poppy shrugged.

'From the days of John the Baptist until now,' Slade looked around as she spoke, 'the kingdom of heaven has suffered violence, Poppy, and the violent bear it away.'

Poppy rearranged the plastic cutlery on her plate.

'They are bringing this to me,' said Slade. 'I can hear them – at night. This is just the last thing in a long-time test of me.' She lowered her voice. 'When I was out there they were everywhere. They put things in my teeth, they can monitor me everywhere. Grace is one of them and enough is enough.' Slade stared at Poppy. 'He told me I needed to deal with it.'

'Jesus?' said Poppy.

'Yes, Poppy – Jesus.' Slade leaned back and looked around again.

It was no use.

'I see your dilemma,' said Poppy.

'Do you?' Slade put down her knife. 'Because to be honest, Poppy, you've been a little disparaging.'

'No disrespect intended,' Poppy said.

Slade looked at her for a moment, 'None taken.'

Dinner was over. All the plastic knives were counted, all the trays were counted, and all the inmates were counted and walked back to their cells.

It happened in the gym a couple of days later. One guard was playing volleyball. The other was outside, sorting something out. Someone smuggled in hairspray, someone else had a lighter. Grace went up quickly. The fire alarms went off, then the sprinklers started. Grace screamed and screamed. Guards came running from everywhere as the sprinklers rained down. No one saw anything and Slade was someone.

The wing was locked down and loss of privileges continued into the weekend. On Monday during lunch Poppy was taken from her cell by a guard who watched her put on a pair of orange overalls over her clothes then led her to the visiting lounge. In the middle of the huge empty room sat her mother and her lawyer, Warren. She hugged her mother and sat down. The guard stood behind them with her back to the wall.

'I told them we wouldn't leave without seeing you,' her mother said. 'It's ridiculous – it's a long drive.'

'It's prison,' said Poppy.

'Warren has some questions to ask and some papers for you to sign,' her mother said.

Warren asked some questions and she signed some papers then he excused himself. The guard radioed for another guard and Warren waited by the door.

'How's Brendon?' Poppy asked.

'Good. I had some photos.' Her mother patted her jacket pockets. 'I'll send them.'

'Cool.'

'Your father put some money in your account. Have you got enough cigarettes?'

'Yes, thanks,' said Poppy. 'Are you going away for Queen's Birthday?'

'No.' Her mother looked around the room. 'Well, maybe, up to Taupo.'

'Nice.'

'Warren said you're back in the sewing room.'

'Yeah,' said Poppy, 'yeah. It's good.'

'You're lucky.' Her mother looked at her nails. 'After last time.'

'Yeah,' Poppy said. 'Unexpected.'

'Well, that'll be good for the money.'

Poppy nodded.

'And the boredom. Idle hands and all that.'

Poppy nodded again.

They sat in silence.

'I'd better go,' her mother said.

They both got up.

'Yeah,' Poppy said. 'Thanks for coming.'

'I'll send the photos.'

'Cool.'

'Might see you for Christmas,' her mother said.

'Cool,' said Poppy. 'Drive carefully. Say "hi" to everyone.'

Her mother sat down as the guard took Poppy to the door, unlocked it and another guard took her back to her cell. She took off the orange overalls and handed them to the guard. The guard closed and locked the door of her cell.

Slade was lying on her bed watching *Dr Ken Agnew*. Poppy said, 'Second opinion?'

Slade smiled and nodded, tapping the remote control on her chin. The camp stretcher was gone.

A month after Grace, Poppy was allowed back on the machines. She made her own mechanical whining to drown out the talk. Two new women started in the sewing room. One of them held the door shut while the other took Slade's eye out with the handle of a plastic spoon sharpened to a point. As the guards broke down the door, the one with the spoon threw Slade on the floor, looked at Poppy, and said, 'Don't think we've forgotten about you, Poppy Tea.' The sewing room was shut for the afternoon.

Poppy was alone in the cell that night. She sat on her bed watching television and listening for the nothing behind the babble. As the lights went out and the television lit the room she thought about her disappointed mother making a cup of tea for her disappointed father. Her brother's birthday was in a couple of weeks. Her mother would make dinner. Poppy had no idea what they would eat or where anyone would sit at the table. She tried to remember the sound of her mother laughing.

Hank Nigel Coolidge

This time it's mist. The woman in the fruit shop calls it 'Scotch mist' because it's 'too cheap to rain'. My grandmother said it was rude to call Scottish people Scotch and for girls to eat on the streets. She said it's unladylike to whistle. Once, I said to her, 'What about giving head?' She pretended not to hear me and I walked away humming something.

I'm walking in the mist, in the morning. I have to walk into it to get wet and the wet sits on me in tiny bubbles so that every time I touch part of me I get wet all over again. I'm also sick. A draining, hacking sick; like the wet parts in my chest are turning to sand. I think I'm dying, but it's nothing serious. Someone's dying – somewhere, someone is really dying, but not me. On the way up the hill I see a huge earthworm. They come out in the rain. I measure it and it's as long as one of my feet and then up to where the stitching starts on the toe of my other boot. It's as thick as my ring finger. It's huge and fat and phallic. I ask it what a nice girl like her is doing in a place like this – on the path in the mist, lying there. I ask if I can buy her a drink. She's coy. I put her in my pocket with some mud and grass, in case she gets hungry. I have to sort of fold her back on herself to make her fit, but I'm gentle, like I'm pulling loose skin off the inside of my mouth. I call her Hank – Hank Nigel Coolidge. I tell her, 'We won't make a habit of this but today you can come to work with me.'

I work in a call centre. I get to my desk, take off my jacket and hang it carefully on the back of my chair. It drips on the floor. Drip. Drip. Drip. I log into my computer, put on my headset and start answering stupid questions – politely. All morning I write, over and over, on my desk pad: 'Mrs Coolidge. Ms Coolidge. Mrs Hank Nigel Coolidge. Dr Coolidge.' I check her every now and then and say things like 'What an idiot' about the people who ring up. They get angry a lot. Our manager gives a prize every week for the best telephone face. The call centre workers stand up sometimes and make claws with their hands and show their teeth at their phones – and talk politely. Our manager tells us people can tell whether we're smiling from the sound of our voices. People come to visit the call centre, clients and our manager's managers, which is why we have to wear corporate casual and be careful when we're making obscene gestures at our phones. As my manager walks past, I ask, 'Are we having "Bring your daughter to work day" any day soon?' He says he doesn't think so and I say, 'Oh, okay, just checking.' He says, great, and there's no such thing as a dumb question.

Hank doesn't eat much at lunch – we go out. She's

starting to dry out. I try to be livelier in my conversation. I talk about the weather and I talk about politics and then I tell her about a TV show I watched the other night about this guy and this other guy and how one of them got smallpox and the other one didn't. I swear I can see a tiny smile on her little wormy face and I feel better.

We get statistics at the end of each day: average time on a call, average unavailable time and any complaints. After lunch my manager calls me into his office. My statistics are down where they should be up and up where they should be down. I say, 'A computer does these – it's all quantitative. You can't judge my performance on that.' My manager shows me a couple of complaints: a lady who said she couldn't understand me, and a man who said he didn't think I was concentrating. I say, 'People take the time to complain. No one takes the time to ring up and praise people. It's human nature.' He shows me the results from my last customer satisfaction survey. There are a lot of numbers and charts, but basically people are not satisfied. My manager explains that the call centre rings these people up. I look through the charts and comments and say, 'This guy thinks I'm okay.' I hold out the paper to show my manager. 'Oh, yeah, there you go,' he says. I tell him I'm having personal problems – that I've started a new relationship and it's not without its challenges. He says, 'That's great' and tells me to forget about all this, he just has to write down that he told me about my performance. Can I sign this thing to say he's told me? I sign the thing. Outside it's stopped raining, it's just grey.

Around afternoon tea time Hank and I start to have problems in our relationship. Hank says I don't excite her any more. I try to excite her. I make faces at the phone – she laughs a little and I wonder if it's enough. She says things like, 'Can we go now?' I try to explain that I need to dazzle them at work for the next little while because my stats are bad and there have been complaints. She says, 'We never go out anywhere any more.' I try to explain the pressures of working in a busy call-centre. She says, 'And, like, I'm not busy too?' I say I value her work and she says, 'You don't even understand my work.' All the time we're having this conversation I'm not taking calls. I've logged myself into 'Unavailable to take calls' status. I watch the seconds tick by on my computer screen. Finally I interrupt her, 'I can't talk about this now.' She says something about me being emotionally unavailable and I zip up my pocket.

On the way home Hank asks if we can have a little talk. My stomach drops. She says, 'It's not you, it's me,' and I start to cry, and say, 'Don't do this – I'll do better, I'll be better.' She asks me to drop her off in the mud beside the path. As I walk away I turn and she's gone, burrowed away from me, and I say, 'I always thought that I'd see you, baby, one more time again.'

A Bad Word

Billy, Maybelline and I drive down from Christchurch. We get to Bonnie and Eddie's at about four in the afternoon. Their son Jet runs to the door to greet us. We put Maybelline on the floor; they stare at each other, then Jet runs away to his room. 'Kids,' we all say and hug each other hello.

That night while we're doing the dishes after dinner, on the outside of the window, which is wet and fogged with the heat from the sink, a white splodge appears. Eddie says, 'Is that snow, or is that sleet?' We look out the window – it's pitch black and Billy says, 'Snow,' and we all agree. We go outside to watch it fall. 'It's like static,' I say. 'What about driving in it?' Everyone nods. The kids have a bath. Bonnie reads Jet *The Tiger Who Came to Tea*. I stand next to the heat pump every chance I get. I make up reasons to stand next to the heat pump that have nothing to do with being lazy and cold. We eat some more and go

141

to bed, and the kids wake up all night with snow jitters.

When the sun rises, the front lawn is white, and the driveway. The hills and the roofs of the houses are also white – like colour's been made illegal. We look out at the snow and some of us move from foot to foot to keep ourselves warm. I put my foot down wrong and almost slip. 'Fuck,' I say. Jet looks at me. 'That's a bad word.' Bonnie says, 'Jet, don't be rude.' We look out on the snow. Everything that was black yesterday is white today.

We decide none of us are going anywhere for a while. We start to see cars moving on North Street and people walking on the footpaths. I can't imagine what could be important enough to bring them out but people are walking on the footpaths. People die in this weather. They go out, slip over and freeze to death. We need food and Eddie needs to pick up a birthday cake for Bonnie from South Dunedin. It's a long way away and Bonnie will worry about him driving, so we mess around home for a while. Billy makes scones with baking soda. Jet likes them. Bonnie and Eddie make wontons from scratch and the sun starts to come up Craigleith Street. The snow melts in some places and not others. Eddie walks out to start his friend's car. Billy does the dishes, Bonnie plays with the kids and I stand by the heat pump.

Bonnie is training to be a dental technician. We used to work together in a library. She makes teeth and eyes. She hasn't made an eye yet but she will, next year. Eddie walks over the icy lawn and down the driveway, kind of kicking his steps, brushing the snow away as best he can before he takes a step – testing each step before he takes it. I've already been out and getting back up the hill was the hard part. It's a favour. His friend left the car here when he went on a trip. Eddie is walking down the icy driveway, slipping a little every now and then, to start his friend's car so the engine doesn't freeze. Eddie and Bonnie's car is on the street. There's no room for it in the driveway since their friend's car is parked there.

People who live here tell people who move here to put socks over their shoes. I have never put my socks over my shoes – I'm not sure it would work if I did. I always thought it was a joke, like, 'Gullible's been taken out of the dictionary.' I've fallen over a couple of times on ice – nothing serious. I've lost control of my car while driving badly: the consequences weren't bad, just the swing the back of it got when I put my brakes on. People tell people who move here not to do that if they hit ice. 'Go with the skid,' they say. You can't see it, that's why they call it black ice. It kills people. Someone dies. They went into the river at Wanaka in their car. The news comes out that it was a Malaysian international student, who Bonnie had heard of but didn't know well. I say, 'It's sad to die so far away from home.' It sounds like the sort of thing I'd heard people say when people died. I regret it immediately.

The church bells ring. All the snow is gone and it is windy and horrible. The kids play and watch the television a lot. We watch a lot of *The Wiggles*. It annoys me. In the afternoon Eddie and Billy go out, under the guise of getting food, to get Bonnie's birthday cake. Bonnie has two birthdays. She was almost a refugee because some countries changed some rules but her uncle bought a fake birth certificate so she has two birthdays – her real one and her make-believe official one. Bonnie says don't

143

worry about the food. I say, 'I'm hungry. Get more food.' After they go and it's just Bonnie and me and the kids I think about the thing I have to do. I don't do it. When they come back they say everyone is buying food – 'It's like Armageddon.' We laugh and eat chips and bread and oil. I hide most of my share from the kids. Billy goes for a walk. I complain because I've been looking after Maybelline the whole time he was shopping but he still goes for a walk. Bonnie cooks, I check my email. Billy and Eddie forgot coconut milk. I say Bonnie should text Billy to get it. He goes to three shops in the freezing cold but no one has it.

We eat the curry without coconut milk. Billy cooks poppadoms and makes the smoke alarm go off. Maybelline eats lots and Jet eats lots and everyone is very happy and full and warm. I clear the table and put all the plates and cutlery in the sink. Eddie does the dishes. Maybelline has a bath and Jet has a shower. Maybelline pisses in the corner by the toys. Bonnie says she's not sure what it is about that corner, but Jet always pees there too. She says 'pees', I say 'pisses', but not before checking Jet isn't anywhere close.

We put the kids to bed. Bonnie reads Jet *Ten Tired Teddies*, Billy sings Maybelline a song and people start arriving. Eddie ushers them into the lounge and I sit with them and we all keep quiet. Eddie goes to say good night to Jet, and Bonnie walks into the lounge. Her eyes get wider and she says, 'Oh, hi everyone.' She has no idea what's going on, it's a surprise, but she's polite. Then Eddie comes back carrying the huge chocolate cake from South Dunedin with candles and we all say 'Happy Birthday'. People have brought other food and presents. After a couple of wines

Bonnie says for her birthday she wants everyone to say what their superpower would be. Someone says, 'Flying.' Someone says, 'I want to be able to get anything I want to come to me – like when I'm on the couch and the remote is on the table, I want to be able to get it without moving.' Someone says, 'Telekinesis.' Bonnie says, 'It sounds like you need a wife.' I laugh and no one else does because his girlfriend is there. Bonnie says, 'Sorry, oh, sorry.' There is silence and Billy asks, 'Bonnie, why do you have two birthdays?' She says, 'I have two names, too.'

Eddie wants everyone to watch a video, but everyone has work or school the next day. I stand by the heat pump for a while. Billy says, 'Have you done it yet?' I haven't. He tells me we're leaving tomorrow, while there's a break in the weather. I go to the kitchen. Bonnie is doing the dishes. There are three piles of white plates with chocolate on them. I say, 'Bonnie,' and she says yes without turning round from the sink. Does she remember the time the money went missing from her purse? When we were working late and everyone said it was me and I said it wasn't. She looks at me over her shoulder and wipes soapsuds around her hands. And I helped her look for the money, behind the couch and under the desks. I say, 'Bonnie it was me,' and here it is, and I hand her an envelope. I say, 'I wrote a note explaining it all.' I hand her the note and the envelope and they soak up the suds as she takes them from me. I say I'm sorry and I'm clean now and thanks for having us. She holds the envelope and the note and looks at me. I look at the envelope and the *B* from where I wrote *Bonnie* disappearing into the water. I say, 'It's all in the note,' and I'm sorry again and the money's in the envelope, I adjusted it for inflation. I'm trying to do better and sorry and happy birthday.

Bleeding

He wasn't feeling well. He hadn't been feeling well for a while. He couldn't remember feeling well, at least not in this financial year, and now this. He was bleeding. He'd tried to rationalise it other ways but, in the far stall of the men's toilet on the fourth floor, there was no denying that he was indeed bleeding. He felt sicker, his cheeks fired up and his mouth went dry and then he said to himself, in his mind so no one could hear, it's probably not as bad as it seems, there is probably a very rational and undisturbing reason for this and he flushed the toilet and washed his hands and went back to his desk.

The day wore on. It became increasingly easy to ignore until he remembered it and when he remembered it it sat on him like a parrot or a ferret. While the others went to a health and safety meeting he googled: *bleeding anus*. He didn't want to but it was talking in his ear, bleating like a sheep. He felt like his cubicle was full of it and it was an

147

animal and another animal and then a flock or a herd or a menagerie. As he looked at the results he asked himself, in his mind, if he was happy now. He asked if *it* was happy now? And it smiled back at him like it was. But, he had to concede that he was not now happy. It said Cancer. Had he lost weight? He looked at his belt and then smiled at his co-workers as they returned and ran his hands through his hair to make it look like he wasn't looking at his belt.

Last week, when he'd dropped his children off, his wife had said, 'You look tired.' He'd looked at her and at Martin, her new husband who was hugging his children, and said, 'Oh, no, you know, work and that.' That was before he'd started bleeding. He wondered how long he should wait. How long was prudent. He pretended to eat his lunch at his desk and read the paper. As he glanced at his computer to see the time, he had new mail. Dorothy Kinbote in Actuaries was going for a drink after work, did anyone want to come. He wasn't hungry but it was a goat. He replied, he was busy and needed to get home, sorry, one of these days, and his email came out, 'Yes, pick me up on your way,' and it was a long slim thing - like a weasel, he suspected. He had never seen a weasel. He may never get to see a weasel.

Dorothy arrived at his desk at around ten past five. He said, 'Oh is that the time?' and carried on typing for a minute. She sat behind him and said no one else could come, was that okay. He said 'Yeah, fine.' He wasn't quite sure who he was but he knew he was still bleeding and as he turned around to her something wise gnawed at his stomach saying, in a calm and quiet voice, 'Maybe you should have called the doctor? Most people I think would have called the doctor.' Her hair was down and she smelled of something not wholly unpleasant. 'Good day?' he said, putting his jacket on as he sat, so he didn't need to stand up with just his trousers on. 'Not bad,' she said, 'better now,' and she smiled and he felt like 135 men afloat on an ice floe. They'd only gone out there for fishing and he was sure they'd been told not to, but then there was a cracking sound and now they would need their cell phones to call for help. Did anyone have a cell phone?

He said he just needed to call his wife, his ex-wife and he phoned her number and she answered and of course he had nothing to say, so he asked about the kids and she said they were fine and was he all right and then he asked about Martin and she said, fine and he said, fine, and then 'Oh, well see you next week,' and he hung up. 'Oh well, that's all done,' he said, moving pens on his desk so they all lined up with his desk pad. 'I guess we can go now.' She smiled.

The pub was warm and full but mainly with people not from his work. There was the odd person but they soon left. He kept his jacket on and got warmer and warmer and prayed the sweat wouldn't break on his face. He went to the toilet occasionally, as little as possible and every time he tried not to think about it and every time he was still bleeding. People didn't go to the doctor for this. Bodies didn't go wrong like this, and if they did his body wasn't going to. His body would go wrong in a lively, romantic way: a broken neck, a lung deflating, a broken heart. Something clean and heroic and worthy of a doctor. What doctor would want to hear about this. It would stop soon. Things like this were private things that went wrong for a week or so and then went right again without anyone having to know. Did he want another drink. Well, he looked at his watch and the dark outside and he started to say he should be heading home, they had work tomorrow and then he thought about home and how there was nothing there but him and his bleeding arse and he said, maybe one more and it patted him on the back and laughed its loud chimpanzee laugh and he laughed along, loudly and hoarsely and she ordered them another drink.

She seemed to be going on a great deal. On and on and on. He was having trouble following her. He hadn't eaten since the bleeding had started. She was talking about something and he was nodding. He would like to have sex with her. He had no idea what part of him would, but something told him he should like to have sex with her. She was talking and he couldn't quite hear her over the noise in his head and the noise of the bar so he nodded and she smiled and nodded some more and he thought this was a way to go. In his head he started making calculations about how much blood he had lost. He wondered if he could claim ACC for something like this, he wondered if he could get condoms and adult incontinence pads at the same place. Equations went through his head as he noticed her pull her bra strap back onto her shoulder. He made containers in his head and tried to remember cosine and tangent and filled the containers with blue liquid and measured them out into cubic centimetres, metres, kilometres – surely not kilometres. She was laughing and smoking. The pub was loud and warm and smoky and he nodded when she nodded and shook his head when she shook her head.

And it said to him with the tapping of a thousand tiny feet that it was only a matter of time. Time, look at the time, would she have another. Go on. Go on. And she will and from the bar he watches her look around the room with the short straw from her drink still between her teeth. He turns too quickly and for a second sees it – all his organs melting and bleeding out of him. His heart bleeding out his arse. His brain. His Achilles tendon. Could he lose blood uphill? Then it was gone and he ordered the drinks and he pulled down his jacket.

Did he want to go dancing? Um, no. Not if she was the last woman alive and the world was an inferno, and the sea and the lakes, and you had to dance to get away. He wanted to have sex with her. She laughs and pushes at his shoulder knocking it off and it has to struggle up the chair leg and back onto his shoulder and it wobbles a bit. He wishes he was bleeding out his face. No, he replies, in her ear, which she has moved to inches in front of his mouth, he did not want to go dancing. He can see the holes in her earlobe where there used to be earrings. He wants to put it in those holes, those tiny half closed up holes. Could he make it small enough to fit? All the worry and the blood, would it fit? And it clatters and runs away to a corner and the bar is getting noisier and hotter and more smoky. She leans back. He says, 'Hospo night.' He doesn't mean to but he says, 'Hospo night.' She doesn't hear him – she keeps talking about dancing. She loves dancing. So he waits until the next time she smiles and nods and he smiles and nods and says, 'Fuck you.' And she keeps talking. 'Fuck me,' he says, and 'Shut the fuck up and suck my dick.' She keeps talking and he wishes she was bleeding from her face. He wishes every one he knew and Martin and some people he suspected he didn't know, he wished all of them would bleed every inside they had out of their faces. And it surprises him, it becomes liquid and long and everywhere, inside everything. He looks around the room and it calls him from everywhere and says it's his brother and it will always be there for him.

He says does she mean dirty dancing and she smiles when he smiles. He leans into her ear again, that ear, and says she's a very sexy lady and she leans into him, the straw still in her teeth and says she's no lady.

As he helps her along the street the two of them get so close he can smell the skin that's flaked from her scalp. She smiles when he smiles. She nods when he nods. It's electric now. He's pissing blood as well. She gets more beautiful with every step. She's licking lipstick from her teeth and his car has dark upholstery.

She stops and bends into a doorway to vomit. He walks on, into the light of a street-light and it scatters and reforms and won't be still.

'Jesus!' she says from behind him, 'Jesus. Are you bleeding?'

He wipes the back pockets of his trousers like he's looking for his wallet.

'Jesus.' She comes over. 'You are. Look at you – you're bleeding like a stuck pig.'

She's close, she smells like vomit.

'You're the pig,' he says.

All at Once

He was happy. It showed in his face. His whole body wore it like a soft layer over what used to be tenseness and bone. Everything about him, his walk, the tone of his voice seemed touched by the one dumb emotion. He held an ugly woman's hand and he kissed her on the cheek. She was the mother and he was the father. The twins took pots and pans from the cupboards of the two-bedroom downstairs flat they rented. He made things stumble now, made them confused. They tried to hurt him and he laughed quietly because he owned them and directed them where he wanted. They were small and obedient in the face of all his joy. They arrested him. Police woke his family in the morning and at night, in the dark. They listened to his phone and talked to his friends and he smiled and relaxed and continued his work in a quiet revolt. He beamed and said hello to the people in the cars outside his home, took them coffee if they worked late and was always full of a lightness that gave him some kind of flight which made him hard to catch and impossible to predict.

She'd saved him twice from drowning. Once in a bath, years before they knew each other. A group of them had set fire to a butcher's shop and gone to a crowded party at a large house to hide They were trying to change everything. She'd shaken him to wake him up and when she shouted, 'Why are you in the bath?' he had no idea. Was he killing himself, did she think? Was the water warm or cold? Was he cooling himself? She said it was cold now but she didn't know how long he'd been there, it could have started warm. She needed to pee. She'd come in there for a pee, could he sit up by himself? Would he prefer to lie down? She put a towel under his head and the colour came back into him.

It should have seemed grand, but if he had drowned, she told him, later, when he tried to make it sound heroic, it would have been a waste, and Frankie and Stella agreed, shaking their small heads and raising their large eyes. He wouldn't tell the story often, just sometimes when he wanted to show how they'd met, how it had been odd – meant to be. How if she hadn't saved him the first time she wouldn't have been there to save him the second time, in the river, when the current took him off his feet, when they were hiding. 'Like Smith's Dream,' he'd say. She would leave the room and he would follow her and she would say it wasn't romantic, it wasn't clever, it was just silly, it was an accident and it happened because he hadn't been paying attention and who knows, maybe if you can change things with your head like her needing a piss at the exact time he was drowning fully clothed in a bath in a big flat, then maybe he wouldn't have even been there in the first place. It was a foolish and a stupid game – infantile. 'It's not even throwing stones at the moon,' she said. 'Who's the romantic now?' he said, reaching for her large hands, hoping the disagreement would end.

There were always people over for dinner; long, involved dinners that started early and went late into the night. People arrived with plates and pots full of food which were laid on a table and, when the table was full, on chairs and on the floor. There was planning and paper, disagreement and finally, always consensus. To begin with she would nurse the twins and they would nod in and out of sleep; now they played at people's feet and climbed the couches around them, saying, 'Can we have some more bread?' and, eventually, someone would take something to the kitchen and find one of them or more often both of them asleep in a corner on top of each other, like mice.

What they were hiding from, in the bush, was a long story. There were snails – and a large coal company. No one believed they could move the snails and keep them alive but that's what the coal company decided to do. There were ten people in Christchurch and they said if anyone from anywhere else could help, it would help. They'd go ahead no matter what, but if others could find their way to the bush where the snails were and build themselves into the trees the coal company wanted to knock down and lock themselves to the earth-moving appliances, it was bound to change something. Slow things up at the very least. There were ten of them, and ten of them could climb ten trees or lock themselves to ten trucks or any combination in between but more people meant more trucks and more tree houses.

They'd left on a Thursday. Nine of them from all over spent the night on the floor of a shared house in Wellington. He was there, crawled into the warmth of the back of her under a couple of sleeping bags they'd opened up, on the floor, like soldiers. They drove to the ferry in the morning dark and as the large boat pulled out, all its lights were weakly on for a moment as a grey dawn came. They lay around outside in the cold wind that came off the capped waves, and ate packed sandwiches, and some of them fell asleep in the laps of others of them, and he talked to his friends and she talked to her friends, and always he would return to her and touch her pregnant stomach and kiss her on the cheek and hug her. They walked around the boat together and from a large glass window they saw cows in a truck and talked about everything that was wrong with everything.

The day the twins were born, winter came all at once, like a heartbeat. The sun set and it was summer and when it rose it was winter, like they'd slept through autumn. She couldn't remember the last time she'd been cold and she felt like she should feel cold now but she didn't, she still felt warm. In the first weeks, she sat on the couch with the babies for hours while he went to work mowing lawns. She would read the babies anarchist manifestos and hum tunes she remembered from childhood. The babies would duck and sway and suckle, making small clucking noises like guinea pigs or something electronic humming away in a room that no one takes notice of except the person who keeps the machines clucking and the humidity low. She would doze, and as her eyes got to the bottom of the page she was reading she would slip into some place that seemed even more real, where the book merged with her life somewhere – a place where she couldn't quite see how everything would turn out for her and everyone she knew.

The coal company security guards came to the clearing in the bush and stood around talking for a while. From high in the trees, they could see them come to a decision. The guards took saws from a vehicle and walked in twos toward the people locked to the earthmovers. While the security guards worked, the people in the trees began to climb down, an inch at a time. Then they jumped and ran for the bush. The security guards looked up from their sawing and then at each other. One of them said something, then another, and they gave chase. If the people from the trees were in the bush but no one knew where, the contractors couldn't start work. There would be an imaginary perimeter where they could pull down trees and where they couldn't. They would have to do the whole thing on estimation – how far the people from the trees could run, whether they would stop occasionally, how much food they had. Wasn't one of the women pregnant? They couldn't run a bulldozer over a pregnant woman, could they?

In the bush, the people from the trees split up. Phil and Rachel would stay close to the edge of the bush but keep moving. It would be nice if the security guards could see them now and then, see Rachel was pregnant, but if not, that was okay. Just keep moving side to side. The others went deep into the bush. Phil wasn't paying attention. He'd stumbled and fallen and somehow fallen into a deep river with a strong current. He'd hit his head and was bleeding. She'd gone in and taken him out. With her super-strength, he would say, with her super-strong arms and her super-strong legs and her special underwater breathing. He came to, wet and laughing, and said, 'I'm like a god,' and for old time's sake and because she was relieved and the relief made her love him, she said, 'You are.'

It was like fire that burned away everything he wasn't using and the clearing it left lasted and lasted all the way through everything. She was the tallest woman he'd ever met. She could lift him like a leaf; he was paper-thin in the bath and for a long time after that. He was paper-thin and angry and all the thinness and anger made him traipse circles into the ground and gave everything against him power. He was drunk, in the bottom of a deep hole in the ground. Some kind of outside hole, he had no idea – it was night, he'd gotten angry and wandered off, climbed a fence and fallen in. After he'd been there for a while, she'd fallen into it too, landing inches from him, spread out with a 'Hoof!' as she hit the damp earth. Was she looking for him, he said as she stood up; she didn't think so. She was looking for something in the sky but the lights in the city were too bright. He said people were looking for him, he could hear them looking for him, if she was quiet for a moment she would hear them, too. They sat and looked out of the hole at the sky and listened and in the distance, and also not so far away, they heard people looking for him. 'That's a lot of people looking for you,' she said. He hated them and he threw his bottle at them without letting go of it and he hated her. 'You're the ugliest woman I know.' She nodded. 'Likewise,' she said. She stopped looking at the sky and stood up to walk around the hole, looking at the walls of it. 'It's like a grave,' he said. She said it was probably to put a pier in; they were building a bridge for the motorway. 'You should have left me in the bath,' he said. She hummed and said probably, and did he want to get out? She could probably lift him up if he wanted to get out. He stumbled up and said for her to leave him and fuck off. She said she couldn't, but she could get him out and maybe he could get someone to get her out. 'You're the ugliest woman I know,' he said again. 'No one's looking for you.' When neither of them talked they could hear the people, still calling his name. 'You're nothing,' he said and threw his bottle again, at her this time, and spirits splashed out. 'I'm the ugliest woman you've ever met,' she said, touching a spot on the wall in front of her. 'I'm like a god,' he said.

'You are.'

'No, I'm like a god.'

'I said, "You are." I'm agreeing with you.'

'I'm like a god,' he said quietly and to the wall of the hole. She tested the spot she'd been looking at as a toehold, and when it held she reached as high as she could above her and pulled herself heavily and noisily out of the hole.

He was sure, but she denied it vehemently, that she

called back into the hole, 'What kind of god are you like, Phil? What kind of god?'

When he went to her the next morning, his face softened and his head pounding, he said, she was right and she told him she had no idea what he was talking about and she kept saying it. She said it now to him laughing at her across the breakfast table while the twins packed their lunches for school. She said he was delusional and she wouldn't have wasted the time once she got out of the hole and why would she waste the time when she was finally out of the hole of the most evil person she knew. He said he wasn't that bad and she said he was, ask anyone, he was angry. 'I was hungry,' he said. She said she wouldn't know about that, and someone had asked if she wanted to be on the Board of Trustees for the school, and he stopped eating and they both laughed. 'You'd be great,' he said, 'you'd need to get a haircut' and they both laughed and the kids laughed. Well, he said, and don't avoid it, she'd thought it, beside the hole, that night all those years ago. But she hadn't, she hadn't thought anything, except: everything needs to change.

A Village

One year we get mice. There is shit and mice everywhere.
I have to sort it out while you go to war to make peace.
Years later, I see you and you're holding a blue beret.
The mice are everywhere. They pop out when I open
doors, move curtains and lift things up. They get in my
hair when I sleep; their tiny, sharp claws get caught and
I have to shake them free before I can get up. When
I shower, five or six of them scurry around the rim
of the bath, covering their eyes. I sing to them. They
have breakfast with me, them, their children and, as the
peace draws on, their children's children. They shred the
telephone book for a bed and we talk for hours. I talk for
hours to mice.

I tell them that M's ute has been parked in D's driveway
all night and that D is away and D's missus is home by
herself. Our next door neighbour works at the Tegel
factory. She shouts a lot. I shout a lot. We don't talk to

each other. Her husband is away, too. Most of the men in our street are away. M is a pogue so he's not away. I wonder how T will feel about his wife being fucked by a pogue.

The mice stop coming around after your friend visits, saying you asked him to do something while you were away. Your friend parks his ute in your driveway for a while and crawls around under your house. He stays for a coffee. While we're sitting in the kitchen having coffee, he looks out the window and says, 'Is that M's ute?' I shrug my shoulders and say, 'I wonder what that's doing there?'

After your friend visits, a bad smell comes from one of the walls. You tell me, what do I want you to do about it from over there, and to call your friend. I call him. He parks his ute in your driveway again and moves the fridge and there's a dead mouse and he picks it up and takes it somewhere. I figure they'll come back now the smell is gone. You come back. I make dinner and you go out and come home and don't say anything and also say you're angry and I'd live in squalor if I could. I do the vacuuming. The phone rings a lot and often it is women asking for you. Some of the women I know and most of the women I don't know. You tell me I'm crazy a lot. I throw things at you. When you go out I just throw things. You cry sometimes. I hide your car keys behind the fridge. I say it serves you right, you shouldn't have done the things that make you cry, and you cry some more. You hit me. I hit you. You almost strangle me one night under a full moon. One of your lungs deflates. It wasn't me – and you still run the Buller half-marathon.

People feel sorry, mostly for me. I feel sorry for me. You go away again and tell me to be gone by the time you come back. You're away for a week. During that week you and your co-workers find a deadly sea snake. You hold it up with a stick for a photograph. After you tell me I feel sick with excitement every time I think about it. I buy a pair of dark glasses. You drive badly and take up smoking. You go for long swims. You can't swim.

Later, years later, the phone rings at 5.30 a.m. It rings again at 5.45, then again at 6.02, 6.09 and 6.12. I don't want to answer the phone. Most companies that run competitions for a lot of money don't open until 9.00 a.m. There are messages – your best friend, then my best friend. At 7.15 I pick up the phone, it's your best friend. I say, 'Oh,' and, 'Oh, well, thanks for calling.' I go to work. I start to shake while I'm typing. The phone rings. It's your best friend, and the army. I say, 'I'm not sure what this has to do with me any more.' And they say I need to be down there as soon as possible and they can organise an army flight for after lunch. I say I wasn't planning on coming down at all and they say I need to come down. I don't think I need to come down. My boss says I need to go home and I say I need to finish the report and she says I have to go home and come back when I'm ready. I say I'm ready now. My best friend meets me at the airport. You slept with her. We drive to her mother's house. I have one bag and we have a cup of tea. I say I don't want to go to your house. We go to your house.

There are lots of people at your house, most of whom I never wanted to see again – all of whom I never wanted to see again. It's a nice house, your house; I imagine you being happy there. It has a nice backyard for running around in, and a fence. You still have the toaster I melted a bread bag to. You were angry when it happened but you still have it – and the coffee mug with the black cat sitting on a patchwork quilt. People say don't I want to see the body. I go to where your body is and that's where I see the blue beret. I look around and everyone seems to be waiting for something, so I cry. I cry in front of a roomful of people who are angry at me. Then and years later, people are angry at me and I am angry at people.

I'm introduced to woman after woman you slept with in cars, at the barracks, in toilets, at our house, at their houses. My father said to me once, 'Oh, that's right, you've never lived in a small town.' You're like a village.

I'm holding a hot cup of tea with no milk, leaning on your bench. One of the women tells me, 'We all thought we were special to him but he loved us all the same. We were all special to him.' I throw hot tea in her face, smash the cup and cut her eyes out – in my head. Someone else tells me you were always faithful; whoever you were with at the time, you were totally loyal to them. I never thought I was special and this is why I think I'm special. I leave. At the top of your driveway there's a drama going on. I'm introduced to your new girlfriend who isn't being allowed in by one of your other girlfriends. It's an odd movement, like a two-handed backhand, but it breaks her jaw and maybe her nose. I spit on her while she's crying and bleeding into her hands. People look. I leave for real. The police call. They tell me it's not okay to hit people. I don't go to the funeral. I lie to my best friend. I tell her that when I get home I'll organise a small memorial service for you. I don't. I'm pretty sure I had no intention of doing it.

You've Come a Long Way Baby

Around lunchtime, I take a walk outside and talk to a bus driver about catching a bus to Bletchley Park. He suggests I take a cab. He says I really want to go on Saturday. On Saturday everyone dresses up and they have a fashion show and bring out the Enigma machine. Or a replica of the Enigma machine, because the original went missing. He says they have old cars on Saturday so I decide to wait because I wouldn't mind seeing some people dressed up.

We're in Milton Keynes. It's a new town. When I ask anyone what it's like to live here, they say, 'It works.' There's one set of traffic lights and not very good buses. The centre of Milton Keynes is the longest shopping mall in the world. The brochure says it was built around an ancient oak tree 'that survives in the food court of the mall'. There's a market in the car park every Sunday and an indoor ski field. In *Strontium Dog* comics, in the future, Milton Keynes is a mutant ghetto.

*

It's a crazy situation. A man rings to ask if Bo and I want an all-expenses-paid trip to England to go to a convention in Milton Keynes. It's crazy even before that, really. They hold an open call for people over six feet and people under five feet. People come and are cast and Bo is cast as the Witch King because he's one of the tallest. They make three movies at once. Film stars, real film stars, come to Wellington and go to restaurants and bars. Teenagers from local schools out shopping meet film stars out shopping. When I look at a map, stretched out on the floor of our flat in Thorndon, I say, 'Look how close it is to Bletchley Park,' and I put one finger on Milton Keynes and another on Bletchley Park and say, 'Bo, is that very far?' because scale gets me confused. 'Do you think I could see Turing's machine, Bo?' I say. 'Sure,' he says, 'maybe.'

We have a week north of London first, in a friend's flat, in a huge tenement block, in Stevenage. People in Stevenage look like they're taking the piss out of themselves. It's chav heaven. There are whole families in shell suits. We catch the train into London, go to galleries and look through the bars of Buckingham Palace. We see squirrels, and marble steps that are worn away by millions of people, over hundreds of years, climbing them. We sleep on the lounge floor and annoy each other – but it's cheap.

On Thursday a black car turns up outside and the driver calls and asks if we can come down because he's a bit worried about leaving the car there. We come down in the piss-smelling lift and he puts our backpacks in the boot of the shiny, black car that local youths are now standing

167

around and shouting at. We get driven to Milton Keynes in the grey cold.

The hotel we're staying in is like *Fawlty Towers*. There are ducks, and people in sunglasses arrive and hug each other. All the way in the car, Bo says, 'Be cool, just be cool.' When the big stars start arriving at the hotel I am very, very uncool. When I say big stars, I mean Giles from *Buffy*, and all the hobbits and people from *Star Trek: The Next Generation* and *Deep Space Nine*. One of the hobbits gives Bo a hug, says 'Boooh,' and pats him as far up his back as he can reach. A taxi arrives, it's the female cyborg from *Terminator 3*. Someone carries her luggage for her. We go to our room and Bo goes for a walk. He says he saw a fox but I highly doubt it. He's nervous. It's all about him. Tomorrow he has to earn our trip to England. At dinner I look around and think, this is ridiculous. I want to say to him, 'Don't be nervous, this is ridiculous,' but I'm not sure whether it would help or hinder.

The next morning a limousine picks us up. We travel with a former child star and his wife who looks like what most people would expect the wife of a former child star to look like. A man who was in *Goonies* with the child star is reading the paper. He starts ripping out an article and says, 'I gotta save this for Benicio – he wants to play Che.' He seems to be saying it to me, so I sort of smile and nod. Nothing in my life has really prepared me for a conversation of this nature.

There are hundreds of people at the mall when we get there. It's a bit of a mutant ghetto welcome. They scream and we get escorted down an aisle between the screaming people. Someone says the hobbits came separately. They're coming round the back while we're coming in the front – we're a diversion.

They haven't opened the mall yet and inside there are tables set up with huge posters above them. One of the women who came with us in the limousine is beautiful; I keep looking at her, thinking she probably plays some sexy vampire or something. She sits under a poster of herself with a Klingon crab-shell on her forehead. George Takei is there and the guy who used to be in *Benson*. Bo gets ushered under a photo of him as the Witch King, which could be anyone. I say, 'Have fun' and they sit the albino twins from the *Matrix 2* on one side of him and Pussy Galore on the other. Then they open the doors.

The idea is that ordinary people buy a photo of the famous person of their choice then get that famous person to sign it. Ordinary people are allowed to take a photo with the famous person as well, so long as the queue's not too long. About ten minutes in they announce they're virtual-queuing for all the hobbits and Giles. I ask someone and they tell me virtual-queuing is when you're given a number and sent away and they call out the numbers over the mall loudspeakers – it keeps the mall clear so if there's a fire or a bomb threat, people will be able to get out. I start thinking about *Dawn of the Dead*. The other friends and partners of famous people seem to know what to do while their famous friends and partners are signing photos and having photos taken. They go shopping and get their hair done and read books in Starbucks. The former child star's wife sits next to him the whole time, rubbing his back. Bo's line is pretty long. He's talking to the guy from *American Werewolf in London*. The twins are wearing sunglasses. They tell Bo it's because of the flash photography. I have another opinion. I take a walk around. I see the oak they built the mall around. I find a grocery store and buy some lunch for Bo, and a coffee. I ask one of the security guards to give the coffee to Bo and Bo smiles, and the security guard says, 'Sorry, no drinks from fans. They have drinks.' I say, 'Oh, cool,' and shrug at Bo.

There are a lot of people dressed in long black coats and others dressed all in white with fangs. I sit down and watch it passing me by. A woman sits next to me, and I say, 'Hi – are you having a good time?' She's beaming. 'Hell yeah.' She has a child with her, a girl of maybe three. The woman has lupus. I'm sorry to hear that. She says that when she was really sick and pregnant, she couldn't move from the couch, and she watched every episode of *Buffy the Vampire Slayer*. 'Giles saved my life,' she says. I say, 'Neat.' She is so excited to see Giles. She's virtual-queuing for him. They're calling 75 – she has 149. I say, 'What do you think your chances are?' and she says, 'Pretty good.' She says neither her nor her daughter would be here if it wasn't for Giles. She took out a £500 personal loan so she could see Giles. She can't wait to shake his hand and she's talked to the security guards about having a photo of him with her daughter. They said she would have to wait and see. She leaves to go and see Buffy's gay friend. I start talking to other people; a lot of them say 'New Zealander!' and I smile and say yeah. I start to feel a little famous myself. I say, 'Oh, I'm married to the Witch King.' And most of them are pretty impressed.

*

I watch Bo for a while. People come up, and he signs their photos and stands up with them for a photo, over and over again. A lot of them go 'Wow' and giggle when he stands up. Some of them tell him he's really tall. When they close the mall doors, he comes out from behind the table and says, 'Those twins have got something about the sunglasses and the flash photography.' I say, 'Only two kinds of people wear sunglasses inside – criminals and wankers.' He has stuff with him. Some Germans wrote him a poem. Germans like him. Some girls from somewhere knitted a scarf for all the hobbits and him. 'There are some pretty weird people here,' I say combing my fingers through the fringe of the scarf. 'Some pretty weird people who paid for our trip,' he says. He's right. I tell him I'm going to Bletchley Park on Saturday and that I can't catch a bus. He finds this hard to believe but I tell him a bus driver told me.

There's a panel that night at a movie theatre. The famous people are going to sit on stage and answer questions and then they'll play the movie, but not before the famous people leave because they've already seen the movie. I can't go because it's sold out, completely, even the aisles. I find myself in a bar, in a multiplex, in Milton Keynes with the hobbits and Bo and Sauron and the other Ring Wraith. Bo says, 'Just be cool, eh?' I am not cool again and giggle a lot and am rude and eventually just sit in a corner. The panel goes well. Bo says they asked him what movies he's working on now and he said, 'None, I'm a librarian,' and people laughed. The hobbits want to go out for a Thai meal. Milton Keynes has one Thai restaurant. We want to go home. We ask if we can go home. I've had enough of the whole hobbit road show. Every now and then I look around and all the hobbits are scruffing each other's hair and jumping around and laughing and I think when I was a kid, and all I wanted to be was special, I would have loved this.

The next day is the same as the day before. I find more food. We don't have a lot of money so I can't go shopping. I sit and watch the people and watch the hobbits. The kid from *Star Wars* arrives – another Kiwi – he's a bit of a shit and is trying to 'pull the birds' as my dad would say. Bo and I say, '*Dead*, hey *dead* – there's someone at the door,' behind his back and slap our knees at how funny we are. I talk to another bus driver who points to a timetable and says, 'You want to catch this bus here and get off it at the indoor ski field, then get on this bus, and the Enigma's not missing it was returned. It's only some bits that are missing.' It sounds bloody confusing but I tell Bo I think I'll give it a go. It doesn't feel like anything can go too wrong in Milton Keynes on a Saturday morning. That night they close the indoor ski field to the public so the hobbits and Boba Fett can go snow-boarding.

The bus thing is confusing. All the time I'm waiting, I'm asking anyone who's around if this is the right place for the bus to Bletchley Park, because I panic when I'm waiting. When I get to Bletchley I have to walk from the town centre. Everything is shut and covered in graffiti like a ghost town – like everyone moved to the mall. I walk down a long, tree-lined lane and at the end there's a sign saying 'Bletchley Park – National Codes Centre'. I pay at the ticket booth and they give me a map and a sticker saying 'Station X'. I follow the arrows that lead me into the huts and out into the sun and back into the huts. They're rebuilding one of the code-breaking machines that Turing and Welchman improved from a Polish plan. It has a room of its own. There's a mannequin standing beside it in a white shirt and a black skirt. She has high-heeled, lace-up leather pumps on and her hair is in Victory rolls. It's a beautiful machine. They have made a beautiful thing for war. I read all the cards on the wall about Turing. None of them say 'gay' or 'court-sanctioned chemical castration' or 'courage under abject cruelty.' They say nothing about injustice and a lot about the glory of the British way of life. I stand back from the cards and take photos of the machine. I take photos until so many Boy Scouts arrive that I can't take a photo without Boy Scouts in it.

The last hut is a computer museum. One of the computers has a cassette deck attached to it and I remember the first time I saw a computer and how it had green writing on a black screen. I remember an ad in my mother's magazines, with a tall skinny woman in flares smoking a slim cigarette. It said, 'You've come a long way, baby.' The boy scouts arrive and start playing *Pong* on the Atari, and more than one of them says, 'This is dumb.'

In the mansion there are photos. Army huts, army vehicles and, standing beside them, all the people no decent person wants to depend on in wartime: people who did crosswords in twelve minutes, homosexuals, pacifists, communists – smart arses. A lot of them look sick and weak dressed in their army uniforms, smoking.

None of them look like they want to be there but all of them are.

In the sun, in the mansion gardens, it looks like every Bletchley local is here, dressed up. There's a policeman on a bike, and women and children milling around. There are no soldiers and I'm not sure how many communists or pacifists. I buy a couple of aerograms with messages in code and post them to myself and Bo in a 1940s post box. There's an announcement that the Enigma machine will be on display in an hour and a half. I decide I can't wait for an hour and a half and get back to Bletchley to catch the last bus, so I buy a postcard of the Enigma machine and leave.

I catch the last bus back to Milton Keynes and the mall. I sit in the mall under the oak and read the brochure from Bletchley Park. The loud speaker says the mall is shutting in ten minutes. I meet Bo, and we get into a limo and go back to Fawlty Towers. The driver passes back an autograph book and says it's for his daughter. I'm the only person in the car who isn't famous. Someone from *Star Trek* says, 'You should sign it anyway,' because not being famous is kind of special in a car full of famous people.

Some of them are going to another convention in Scotland, another mall. Bo and I are going to Paris, on a train where no one recognises him. We get a room on the top floor of a hostel. If you lean out the window you can see the Eiffel Tower. Bo leans out the window and tries to take a photo of himself and the Eiffel Tower but his head gets in the way. That night, before it gets dark we sit by the Seine and watch a small dog play with the

174

body of a headless pigeon. 'Alan Turing killed himself with an apple,' I say to Bo as we watch the dog. 'Like Snow White,' he says, and I say, 'Yeah.' The dog kind of throws the pigeon, what's left of the pigeon, in the air a bit. 'Or Adam,' I say.

Shopping

May's mother, Jane, walked toward the car, lighting a cigarette in the wind. It looked like she was holding something in front of her face with both hands; something small and soft, like a kitten. May had never seen her mother holding a kitten. They'd had a cat. It had been their neighbours', they'd fed it in the holidays and the neighbours said to May, 'It likes you so much. You should keep it.' He was a large ginger cat called Tiger. May would call him, and hit the cat food tin with a spoon so it made a dull bang-bang noise. She was sure her mother had killed Tiger. Jane denied it but May remembered coming home in her green and white school uniform and brown Roman sandals to find Tiger gone. It was always summer in May's memory. So hot she didn't need to wear a cardigan; always in Roman sandals or bare feet. Her mother said she didn't know where Tiger was and sometimes cats just crawled away to die.

There was a lot of cat food left. May's cousin offered May's brother five bucks to eat Tiger's food. Not all of it. They agreed a tablespoon of cat food for five dollars and shook on it. Her brother ate it but it turned out their cousin didn't have five bucks. At a family meal, when they were teenagers and someone was telling the story, her brother said, 'Yeah, what about my five bucks?' Their cousin shrugged and everyone at the large family table laughed except May, who said, 'What about Tiger?' The laughing stopped, not because everyone knew what had happened to Tiger but because they knew Tiger always started a fight between May and her mother. Almost everything May said started a fight with her mother; she was always trying to start fights. May's father, Gavin, laughed to himself and said, '*What about my five bucks?*' Everyone laughed again, only not so loudly. At the hospital, during family counselling, May's mother said, 'You never even had a pair of Roman sandals. I hate Roman sandals.' She said it was all in May's head – all of it.

May wanted to say, 'You can't smoke that in here,' but she got into the car and waited pretending to read the shopping list over while Jane finished the cigarette. May and her mother were going shopping for food for Finnegan's first birthday party. Jane had given Finn a card saying 'Happy Birthday Darling, You are so lucky to have such fantastic parents.' She meant May and her husband. Jane bent down and stubbed the cigarette out in the gutter. She got in the car and said, 'This is nice,' and squeezed May's knee. May smiled and started the car. They hadn't spent time alone together for years.

Every time a car came close Jane inhaled swiftly, realised, and tried to cover it up. They were driving May's father's car. He held the keys out to May, thought better of it, and gave them to Jane. As they walked down the path, Jane put the car keys in May's palm and said, 'You drive, eh? You know the way,' then, almost immediately, 'Oh, my wallet. I'll just go back for it.'

'Nice day,' May said as they came to a stop at some traffic lights.

'Yeah,' her mother looked out the window. 'Let's hope it holds up for the party tomorrow.'

May nodded.

'How many kids are coming?' Jane said.

'I'm not sure.'

'Oh well, I'm sure if we get enough food for twenty that should do it.' Her mother put both hands between her legs and pulled her shoulders up to her ears. 'Shouldn't it?'

The supermarket car park was busy and the sun was glinting off all the cars.

'Should have come earlier,' Jane said.

May parked the car.

In the fruit section Jane said, 'Strawberries.'

May took the shopping list out of the back pocket of her jeans and said, 'I have a list.'

Her mother stood beside the trolley holding the strawberries. 'Does the list have strawberries on it?' she said.

May looked at her then looked at her list and they both laughed.

'Strawberries do not appear to be on the list,' May said.

'I can change that.' Jane opened her bag, looking for a pen.

They both laughed again.

'We can't really afford them,' May said.

'I can afford them. This shop's my shout.'

'That's kind but we have money for the shopping.' When she had wanted to put it right, May added up all the money she owed her parents and it came to eight thousand dollars. She made an appointment to see her father. People told her he would probably say, 'Don't be silly. It's just great you're doing so well.' When May showed him the figure, itemised into money stolen, fines and bills paid, her father said, 'That should just about do it.' He gave her a bank account number and said if she could organise a direct debit, that would be fine. May got a job in a fast food restaurant and when it was all paid back she was invited to Christmas dinner. Gavin and Jane handed May an envelope and in it was a cheque for eight thousand dollars. May and her father did the dishes, and while Jane was in the back yard having a cigarette, he said, 'Don't fuck up,' and he meant it.

'We can go halves,' May said. She wanted her mother to tell her she was doing a good job of looking after her family but more than that she wanted to get the shopping done, and she didn't want to fight.

Jane put the strawberries in the corner of the trolley, 'All right,' she said, 'but I'll pay for the strawberries.'

They began to get the things on May's list: oranges, bananas, apples. May read from the list and Jane went to the shelves and picked the best fruit and put them in the trolley, carefully, keeping the strawberries in the corner away from everything else, like they'd been naughty.

'Do you have to weigh them?' her mother said as May put the bags of fruit on the scales. 'I don't shop at this one.' Jane looked around nervously at everyone shopping.

'What about chippies?' Jane took a packet off the shelf.

May looked at her list, and they both laughed.

'Well, I want some chippies,' Jane said and grabbed a couple more packets. 'And some dip.' She put the chips next to the strawberries. 'Don't let me forget dip.'

In the baking goods aisle, while she was looking for lemon essence, May realised she'd lost her mother. Jane had gone to get some olives – they were on the list but they'd missed them at the deli. She'd been away too long for just olives. May looked around, holding the small bottle of yellow liquid. She put the lemon essence in the trolley then went to the end of the aisle; her mother was looking at basmati rice. 'It's really cheap here,' she said. 'I might start coming to this one.' Her mother was carrying a small plastic container of olives and a white plastic bag. 'This is cheap, do you need rice?' May shook her head. Her mother put the rice back on the shelf and put the olives in the trolley. She held the plastic bag close to her and whispered, 'Some ham – for your dad's lunch.'

'I was going to make lunch,' said May.

'I know.' Jane jumped a little bit without leaving the ground. 'It's just extra. I can put it back.'

'Don't put it back.'

'I'll put it back, eh?'

'Nah, put it in the trolley.'

'But you've made lunch.'

'I haven't made lunch. I was going to make lunch. We'll have sandwiches.'

'I'll put it back.' Jane walked away.

May watched her talking to the man behind the deli counter. She handed the plastic bag over. The man shook his head and frowned. Jane smiled and waved and, as she turned toward May, laughed and said, 'No problem.'

May looked at her list as they joined the check-out queue.

'Dip!' her mother said, raising her hand. 'I wanted some dip.' She darted off toward the fridges. May looked at her watch. They'd been gone nearly an hour. May had used the eight thousand dollars to finish her degree. Gavin hired a suit to wear to her graduation. Jane had stood in front of her, fiddling with the collar of her shirt, trying to get it to sit under the strap of the hood, then over it. Her mother looked down through the bottom of her glasses, concentrating only on the collar. Finally, she patted it and said, 'That'll do. That looks okay.' Jane tried to look down at the collar, then touched it. 'Thanks,' she said.

Daisy

Daisy liked to push the trolley. She would push it forever if she could – to the coast. But her mother or father would always pick her up and turn her back on her path. She would keep pushing, and walking her little side-to-side steps, thinking she would push forever in the new direction, but soon she saw the gate and home. Her mother or father would open the gate and she would turn the trolley in a banging, scraping arc, up the path to the steps that led to the door. Her mother or father would lift her into the house, Daisy still holding the trolley, and she would push it some more, up and down the hall, into the bathroom and behind the curtains that hung to the ground.

The trolley had been built by someone else's grandfather in a workshop lit by a single bulb. He'd purchased the wood from a small store he could walk to but he'd had to catch a bus for the wheels. Yellow plastic wheels that rattled, and wobbled slightly. When he found them he held them up and said, 'These are them.' On the bus home he took them from the bag and held them again and thought, 'They're as close to perfect as you get.' The nails that held them on were rusting now from puddles and rain. The tray lay low to the ground and the handle came out at a forty-five degree angle. Daisy's mother bought it from a shop full of old things, along with a bucket and a wooden chair, but Daisy had found it – tucked away between an old bath and a rusty bike. She pulled and pulled and the trolley popped out. She'd fallen to sitting, a hard fall that stopped abruptly and clamped her teeth together, but she wasn't down for long. There was dirt in the corners of the tray, crushed as fine as sand. Daisy pinched at the grains with her tiny fingers, then wiped at them swiftly with a flat hand, but they never went away. She pushed the trolley a little from her sitting position and it rolled away, so she got up quickly and began pushing it, both hands on the handle, laughing in a 'huh-huh' way. Daisy thought it had been left there for her. She didn't know about giving things up or getting taller. She was small, not two years old, and everything was there for her.

At first, in the confines of their small house, Daisy got the trolley stuck constantly. She would push it forward a few steps and its corner would catch on a chair leg or the edge of something bigger. She would push and push harder and sometimes the back wheels would leave the ground and Daisy, still holding the handle, would fall face first, then kneel to save her face and she would cry – cry out. Her mother would wipe her hands on a tea towel, saying 'It's okay,' and as she lifted Daisy and put the trolley on a clearer path, 'sometimes these things happen when you're pushing a trolley, but it's okay, it's all part of pushing a trolley.' Daisy's mother, Alice, was always busy.

One Monday, Daisy turned the trolley for the first time. It got stuck and she pushed and pushed and then pulled and it came free. She shook it then pushed it again and all the sticking places disappeared.

Daisy sometimes stopped pushing to watch her mother being busy. Eventually, as the busy-ness went on, she would raise her arms and call out. Alice would hand her down a piece of pumpkin, slimy at one end and tough at the other. Daisy would play with the pumpkin for a moment; pushing her finger as far into the slimy end as possible, then she would look at her mother and go to the wooden chair her mother had put beside a Formica table. Daisy would drop pumpkin on the rented carpet, leaving another orange thumbprint, and hit the seat of the chair with both hands, saying, 'Ah, ah.' Alice would try not to look up. If she could just finish cutting the pumpkin for the soup for her friend who had twins who both wanted feeding at the same time but could only be fed one at a time. Then she would play with Daisy. Alice tried not to look up and chopped the pumpkin on the board with the seeds caught in a slimy, orange net. 'Ah, ah.' Alice chipped at the green skin like a sculptor working limestone. 'Ah – ah!' Alice looked up.

Alice would fill the sink with bubbles and plastic cups and Daisy would eat the bubbles and spill the water, but she wanted the knife. Alice would chop on the glass chopping board and it would make high-pitched bangs like something was about to break. Of everything on the bench that she could have and everything on the bench she couldn't have, it was the knife Daisy wanted most. Alice dreamt when she was awake and in one dream she would, in some strange mind, hand Daisy the large chopping knife, put her on the floor to play, and turn back to her cooking. Daisy would run away up the hall and trip on the threshold to her room. The knife, at an impossible angle, would puncture her cheek and her skull and somehow her heart, and she would not call out. Her mother would sauté the onions and garlic, add nutmeg and stir the pumpkin into the sizzle at the bottom of the big pot. She would think, it's calm and peaceful – the way it used to be - and add the stock. When it came to a boil and she'd put the pumpkin skin, green and chipped off, in the bin and cleared the bench, she would see the knife was missing and think, Where is Daisy? Alice would see the trolley in the lounge and think, that's odd, and look up the hall and see the fallen girl. She wouldn't see the pool of blood until she was standing over her. She made it all in her head; her stomach was a knot of fear as she did. So Alice stopped chopping, filled the sink, pulled the wooden chair to the bench and stood Daisy up on it, putting the chopping knife well out of reach.

Later, after they took the pumpkin soup to the friend, and Daisy had seen the twins and tried to roll her trolley over them both, one at a time, she found the pumpkin under the Formica table and put it in her trolley with the two potatoes, the plastic bottle full of rattly chickpeas and the plastic keys she took to her bath each night – in the morning too, if she got porridge in her hair. She could hear the gate from anywhere in the house. When the metal bolt slid it squeaked, and Alice would shout, 'Who's that?' with equal excitement every night. 'Daisy? Who's that?' Sometimes Alice would cover her mouth with both hands, like she was praying, and open her eyes as wide as they would go. Daisy would run to the front door, she would reach for the key inside and try and Alice would call from the kitchen, 'Don't stand too close, Puss. Stand back.' The door would open and it would be her father, Lucas. He lifted her up so she could play with the headphones that hung on cords from the collar of his jacket. He would kiss her and kiss her and kiss her again. His cheeks would be cold. Daisy would smile but not look up, as if the smile, like everything else, was there just for her. Lucas would take her to the bedroom and put her on the bed and she would crawl over and reach for the remote and turn on the television and laugh, 'Huhuh.' Lucas would change out of his suit and shout, 'How was your day?' Alice shouted back, 'We had fun, we visited the twins and Daisy pushed her trolley, we had a good day.' Then Alice would come into the bedroom, wiping her hands on a tea towel, and Lucas would kiss her and say 'Nice to see you.' Alice would say, 'What are you watching, Puss?' and Daisy would look up and smile so wide her nose would scrunch and her eyes would squint. Lucas would look at her and giggle. He was glad it was over.

Sometimes it felt like Daisy had been awake the whole first year. It felt like no one had slept and all three of them had gone a special kind of crazy. Crazy like they were too tired to be sane. He'd broken a couple of his fingers when she was three months old. He was in a hurry and he'd slipped on grass growing through paving stones. Grass wet at lunchtime because it was August and there was no sun to dry it. He stood up and his hand ached and his arm ached and he felt dizzy and sick with the pain. An ambulance was called. He'd pleaded with them not to call an ambulance but an ambulance had been called. His little finger was dislocated and the two next to it were broken. They gave him nitrous oxide and said, 'Are you ready?' He said, 'Is it going to hurt?' and they said, 'He's not ready.' At the same time one of them dropped a book. Lucas jumped as the book hit the floor and the doctor cracked it back and Lucas jumped again at the pain of his smallest finger being snapped back into its socket. He'd called Alice when he could. They were going on a plane that night. Not a long trip - it was for Alice's birthday, to visit her parents. He'd been getting her a present when he fell; he was late for a meeting. He thought he could make it to the shop and back but he was late for the meeting and he ran and he fell and he'd broken two fingers and dislocated one and could she come and pick him up from A & E? They decided to go anyway; Alice's parents could help. Daisy cried the whole way up in the aeroplane and someone complained. Alice got angry at the complaining person and at Lucas, who was in too much pain to get angry and should have got her present earlier and not been running. Lucas sat in the seat in the plane, wishing with everything he could muster over the pain and the exhaustion that he could go back and not run and not fall and not let Alice down on her birthday. He was glad it was over and Daisy was smiling her scrunchy-faced smile. Alice tried to do one too and Daisy laughed and soon all three of them were scrunching their noses up and squinting their eyes and smiling as hard as they could.

On Saturday mornings it was all three of them for a while after breakfast. Daisy would eat her porridge and her toast and put her banana beside her on the high chair. If no one was looking she would put porridge in her hair and in her ears and in her eyelashes and brows. She had a bath. If she was quick she could get the banana back before her chair was tidied away and walk around in just her nappies, eating banana and squashing it in her hands. Sometimes she would help clean up with the yellow and white cloth that she could suck and suck and sometimes get the taste of bubbles out of. She would go to her trolley, take out the potatoes and the chick-pea bottle and put them on the floor beside it, then go to the bath and fish out the plastic keys and put them in her trolley. Daisy would check the level of the dirt in the corners of the tray and if it was low she'd go to the large potted plant beside the bookshelf, put her hand flat on the dirt, then pull her fingers into a fist and take some dirt back to the trolley. She'd rub one hand on the other and wipe dirt into the tray of the trolley until the grains were fine. Then she would put the potatoes into the trolley, one by one, and finally, shaking it to make the chickpeas rattle loudly, she'd put the bottle back, always at the top by the handle. If it looked under-loaded she reached up and grabbed whatever came to her hand on the Formica table to put it in the trolley as well. Daisy pushed her trolley to the door and reached for the key and looked behind her for Alice or Lucas and if no one was there she would reach harder for the key and shout, 'Uh, uh,' until someone came and said, 'We're not going out at the moment.' Daisy would say, 'Uh, uh,' as if she felt they didn't understand her. When they walked away, she would stamp her feet and cry out as loud as she could, 'Uh – Uh!'

This Saturday Lucas came back, holding a cardigan knitted in light blue wool with a hood and large buttons. Alice came next, her jacket on, holding a pair of outside shoes for Daisy. Daisy leaned on Lucas's legs while she lifted one foot then the other to be shod, like a horse.

'You need to go backwards so we can open the gate,' Alice said. She had a bag on her back. Daisy had the trolley pushed right up to the gate. Alice's bag had a bell on it and a zip and Daisy had put a small plastic Alsatian in it last night before her bath.

Daisy loved to push her trolley. She stopped under a large gum tree and looked up at tui playing in the branches. The bark on the trunk peeled like a potato. Daisy squatted, picked up a piece of bark and put it in her trolley next to the water bottle Alice had added as they left. Then she stood, leaned back and watched the birds again. This is what it would have looked like from the road. A tall man, a short woman and a toddler, all heads leaned back looking up into the branches of a gum tree. The tui flew away and Daisy took up pushing again. She felt like she could push forever. Just past the shops, Alice started saying, 'Bye, bye, Daisy,' and Daisy stopped and looked up at her from under the brim of her hat. The sun was out but there was no heat in it yet. Alice leaned down and kissed Daisy on the cheek. 'Bye bye,' she said. Lucas leaned down and kissed Alice on the cheek, 'Bye

bye.' Alice turned and walked away. Daisy stood, both hands still on the trolley, watching Alice walk away. She looked up at Lucas and pointed at Alice. Lucas said, 'Bye bye, Alice.' She looked back and Alice was gone. She was standing around the corner of the dairy waiting, crying a little; her throat and eyes filling. This time, like every time, feeling like the last time she would see her daughter. Alice peeked around the corner and Daisy was looking up at Lucas with one hand on the trolley handle and the other held out, opening and closing, into a fist, saying, 'Eye. Eye liss.' Then Daisy turned and pushed her trolley towards the park.